THE THAT READS THE READER

surprising, shocking, amusing and surreal short stories

John Smale

revised and with even more stories, replacing:
THE BOOK THAT READS YOU
by John Smale

Published in November 2020 by emp3books Ltd
Norwood House, Elvetham Road, Fleet, GU51 4HL

©John Smale 2020

ISBN 9781910734360

Some parts of this book were previously published as THE BOOK THAT READS YOU, ISBN 9781910734322, in 2019

For more information about this book or others, visit www.emp3books.com

The author asserts the moral right to be identified as the author of this work. All views are those of the author.

All rights reserved. No part of this publication may be reproduced, stored in a retrieval system, or transmitted, in any form or by any means, electronic, mechanical, photocopying, recording or otherwise without the prior written consent of the author.

Limit of Liability/ Disclaimer of Warranty. Whilst the author and publisher have used their best efforts in preparing this book, they make no representation or warranties with respect to the accuracy or completeness of this book and specifically disclaim any warranties of completeness or saleability or fitness of purpose. Neither the author nor the publisher shall be liable for any damages, including but not limited to special, incidental, consequential or any other damages.

All names are fictional and do not refer to any person living or dead. The same applies to places, buildings and any location.

Cover designed by killercovers.com

BOOK REVIEW
from Mensa Magazine

What if your book could read you...

Imagine, if you will, that you pick up a book and start reading...and the book starts reading you...

It knows instantly your story, all your secrets, your thoughts and deeds, right down to your very soul.

"You think you are reading me. You are, but I am also reading you. I am inside your head. It's an interesting place to be, to be honest."

That is the surreal and engaging scenario created in this quite wonderful work, penned by Mensa member John Smale.

It is a vehicle that allows the book (writer) to tell a collection of what could be seen as short stories but definitely with a twist.

There is the battered wife and a happy ending...the innocent man in jail, framed by his wife and her gangster lover...who get their just desserts...the old man with dementia in a care home who knows more than most people think...and the priest who dies in a very surprising confessional moment...

This is a brilliant book. The stories would very much have stood up as a collection of work in their own right but the extra and imaginative addition of the idea that there is a book that reads people adds to the brilliance.

If you like stories with a twist, ones that reveal the vagaries of life in all it many forms then this is definitely for you.

Very highly recommended.

Brian Page, editor of Mensa Magazine

CONTENTS

1	SHORT STORIES FROM AN UNUSUAL AUTHOR	1
2	BREAKING NEWS	3
3	THIS BOOK IS FOR, AND ABOUT, YOU	7
4	A DEADLY RED HEART	11
5	JUDGE AND JURY	19
6	PARALLEL LINES	21
7	BEYOND CARING	25
8	COPY AND PASTE	29
9	DYING FOR A DRINK	37
10	MISREADING PEOPLE	40
11	DIRTY BOOKS	46
12	IN THE NICK	50
13	INDIAN TAKEAWAY	56
14	OUT OF PRINT	64
15	TWO SIDES TO EVERY STORY	68
16	MOANER	75
17	LOST FOR WORDS	79
18	SEEKING HIS DESTINY	83
19	THE EMPEROR'S WINE	87
20	DIRTY, MUDDY CORPORATE TRENCHES	91
21	THE COFFEE TABLE	98
22	CONFESSIONAL	104
23	RICH AND POOR	108
24	MAKING AN EXHIBITION OF HIMSELF	114
25	THE PAIN OF DEATH	118
26	GARDEN OF ADAM	122
27	THE BIRDS AND THE BEES	128
28	ANN ADIEU TO A FRIEND	132

29 OUT OF BODY AND OUT OF MIND	134
30 THE TROPHY BRIDE	141
31 SO TIRED OF WAITING	145
32 JAMIE	147
33 THE VETERAN	151
34 GIVING TOO MUCH	154
35 HER DISCOMFORT ZONE	157
36 WRONG AND WRITE	159
37 LITERARY CRITICS	162
38 THE DREAM MAKER	164
39 FIRST AND LAST LOVE	167
40 SWEATING IT OUT	170
41 A GHOST MADE HER SLEEP WITH A MAN	182
42 A DEAD-END OBITUARY	186
43 PREDATORS AND PREY	189
44 A CUT ABOVE THE REST	192
45 LIFE IS LIKE A SIMILE	195
46 EIGHTEEN EIGHTY	197
47 THE THERAPIST'S THERAPY	199
48 REACHING A VERDICT	202
49 CLOSED BOOK	206
50 WHAT ABOUT YOU?	207
REVIEW REQUEST	209

Other books by John Smale
All available as paperback, Kindle and audiobooks.

Moving Forward
We have all made mistakes that have held us back. When we know what went wrong for others, then we can avoid problems and move forwards in our lives. Although some might be upsetting, these stories and metaphors help the readers to climb out of the sticky mud that holds them back and delivers them into a place where they can be fulfilled and happy.

Mind Changing Short Stories and Metaphors
Metaphors are the paints that illuminate a black and white drawing. They are mirrors of the mind. The face you look at in the mirror is never the face others see, but when we look at ourselves from a different viewpoint then we can see the changes that will make us better.

Short Stories and Metaphors
Following his decades in advertising, marketing and as a fully trained and very experienced hypnotherapist, John Smale has put together a number of stories and metaphors that have worked to help people to resolve a huge range of problems.

STOP believing the lies, BELIEVE IN YOURSELF
The formula for rescuing your self-belief, esteem, confidence, worth, love and happiness
The highly effective method for building self-esteem, confidence and self-help with emotions. This self-belief book explains in a straightforward manner why many people feel they have failed and shows how they can be successful and happy in their lives by recovering the self-assurance they should have.

1
SHORT STORIES FROM AN UNUSUAL AUTHOR

Never misunderstand what I, this book, can and cannot do. It is not a quiz that will tell you things about yourself as you will see in some magazines. You should know more about yourself than a simple questionnaire will expose in any case. Having said that, I know a lot about you already.

So dear reader, this is my narrative about the lives of others that I became aware of when they read me. It is just a kaleidoscope of stories showing different natures of people in a random way. Each story is short but complete.

It has been said that I am like the 'invisible' villain in a crime story. The postman or the waiter who is taken for granted and who can see what is happening but remains unseen until exposed.

I will emphasise that I am an observer, not a voyeur.

Let's get poetic and describe the scenery, the birdsong, the smell of cut grass and all of that stuff. Maybe not. Forget that. I am a book. I have no senses of my own so do not expect bodice ripping tales or zombies ripping people apart. I am like a prism. I take one light, the human population, and split their collective accounts into different stories that liberate their innermost thoughts for you to enjoy.

I am a book, yes, a simple book and as I said already, without the ability to see and feel thoughts, emotions and intentions. I borrow those from my informers. Otherwise, like books on a shelf I just sit but, when I am picked up by a person, I know everything about them.

The cover on my earlier edition had a man's eye on it but there was no sense of identity, and I am told that it scared people. This book has a totally different one that is hopefully more pleasing to the eyes of the reader.

I have no gender and my stories are about both men and women. Laugh at some, cry at others but above all be entertained by a different perspective on the lives of others.

And if you need to package me into a category, people have tried to define my genre. Horror, comedy etc. You decide because life cannot be generalised into a labelling system.

I make no money from these books because I do not need any. The printer and retailers take their shares. And, please be aware that I am not a gossip. I enjoy telling tales like the old storytellers in the past who would sit around fires and fascinate the audience.

Some of my tales are perhaps funny, others sometimes sad. Most of all they are to meant to provoke your thoughts and emotions as they reflect what I have gathered from the previous consumers of my observations in my other books.

We all like to know the distasteful secrets of others but it can be difficult to get them at first hand. Yet, something seemingly detached and innocent can be the receptacle and the exposer of those hidden truths about lies. Most of us will know that with other people we hear the stories they want to share but not the ones they want to forget.

Your story is hidden but, for others their tales are an open book for all to see. I will tell you a great deal, including how I, a mere book, killed a person. And there are stories about gender changes, criminals, cheats and lovers, to one about a man who tricked his way into a care home, fell in love and got thrown out. These are just an introduction to lots and lots of a huge variety of short stories.

So, in this book, there are light and dark thoughts for you dear reader, and many hues in between.

Let me tell you more.

2
BREAKING NEWS

…. I need you to hold on for a while, dear reader. Something has happened to another reader and I need to help.

A woman called Lucy has been attacked by her partner, Brian. He picked me up and started calling her stupid because she was paying too much attention to me and not to him. This has been a repeating pattern in their relationship. He wanted her to give him all of her time. He needed her to be like his mother was when he was a toddler, looking out for him, looking after him, devoting all her time to the spoiled brat as I can read him as being. I know them both very well.

She is a beautiful woman who shines kindness and generosity of spirit through every pore of her body. She had never enjoyed the wild life and after a few serious boyfriends, had reserved her love for the man she had met and married. That evening, she had cooked an excellent meal which reflected his favourite foods and having cleared up, she sat to relax with a book, me, as it was. An innocent looking paperback that did not divulge its secret ability to reach inside the reader. Funny in places, she laughed now and again and he reacted as if he had caught her with a lover.

Long before the events that would bring matters to a head, and an end, she was upset. She had become very unhappy after meeting what she thought was a perfect man who had manners and charm. When the wrapper fell off him, the true nature of the guy became all too apparent. He had bullied his mother with threats and violence that she could not recognise as such. He would bite her and, when she got angry, he said he would run away and die. He was a little monster even at the age of five.

Back to what has come to pass. He had thrown me at her. 'Lucky it was the soft paperback rather than the harder Kindle.' He had laughed as I hit her eye. She screamed as he rushed towards her with his fist clenched. 'Give me a new bruise to match all the others.' She shouted. I could feel her fear. He had bullied her verbally, emotionally and physically. She had to lie to her friends in order to stop Brian from hearing about what was going on in her life third hand. His intimidation was powerful enough to make her worry that he would kill her. He had told Lucy that if she left him then he would track her down, tie her up and burn her to death. Her greatest dread was being burnt.

I promise you, dear reader, I did not do it on purpose, I am unable to move, but as he got near Lucy, his foot slipped on my shiny and glossy cover as I laid on the floor. As he fell, his head smashed against the coffee table and he lost consciousness. His blood flowed onto the floor. Lucy froze as she looked at the man she had once loved, dying. Rather than call for an ambulance she made herself some strong, sweet tea and sipped it slowly. He was impotent now, unable to carry out any threats. She looked at the reddening of the tweed his jacket was tailored from and she recalled how he had persuaded her father to pay for clothes that he would wear to match the beauty and radiance of his daughter.

Now he was dead or dying, Lucy ran through all the horrible things that had happened to her at the hands of the corpse on the floor. She smiled, felt guilty but smiled again.

She picked me up from the floor and said 'thank you.' With that moment, all of her emotions flooded into her mind and were transmitted to me. I was not a murder weapon; I had been a third party to the death of a nasty man. What I had read in him when he had picked me up to throw at Lucy told me so much about how he had spent his life as two people. The charmer who could get his own way with his mother and other women he had met, but he was also an oppressor and tormenter who delighted in hurting others when they did not follow his plans for his own pleasure.

He had been perfect at the beginning. Compliments flowed as easily as his blood did now. He took her to the theatre, bought expensive dinners and when she had fallen for him, they had the perfect life of love, tranquillity and shared interests. Her parents were not rich but financially comfortable and he wanted a share of what they had.

She agreed to his proposal of marriage and the wedding went without a hitch until the honeymoon night when he started making demands that were not to her liking. He seemed to want to make love like an animal or a porn star. She resisted, called him a pervert and he hit her for the first time. The following morning, she explained the bruise on her cheek by saying that she had tripped after drinking too much champagne.

The pattern was set. If she said no to anything, he would throw things at her or punch where the marks could not be seen. She hated him. He was so different, but she was trapped. The one time she had told him she wanted a divorce he held her head under water in the sink until she passed out. When she came to, he told her to apologise or have a repeat of what he had done.

He had, in the past described their relationship as, the alpha male stuck with his 'little lady'.

And today, after the paramedics had declared him dead and the police arrived, I was unable to be a witness obviously, but they were able to figure out what had happened anyway.

Just now, Lucy washed a few splatters of blood off my cover and put me onto her bookshelf. Why she kissed me is not really a mystery.

Going ahead now, after the inquest she collected his personal effects. Shocked and surprised at first, but not after thinking about it. She was given two packets of condoms, something he never used with her as she was on the pill. Then his wallet that contained photographs of a variety of women, all in the same pose, bearing their breasts at the camera. She was told by the police that his phone had similar images except that they showed the women totally naked and there were lots of shots of him without clothes that he must have sent to them. She did not want his phone or the images and she tore the photographs into pieces and threw them in the bin. The letters from his credit card companies were horrific. He was overspent on three cards and the amount of money he must have spent would have financed a lifestyle of a rich playboy, which is the life he played out.

'So much better off without him.' She shouted as she wiped tears from her cheeks.

3
THIS BOOK IS FOR, AND ABOUT, YOU

Sorry for the interruption but I needed to tell you what has just happened although the times were a little distorted.

Dear reader, back to an explanation about a book that reads people. I have no idea how or why it happens but I will do my best to explain what I know.

You think you are reading me. You are, but I am also reading you. I am inside your head. It's an interesting place to be, to be honest.

I can see you raising your eyebrows, by the way.

What you say out loud and what you think are different. Your views are given to you by others. There is little that you have discovered or invented that is new apart from with your emotions. You process the flood of information that has been delivered to your mind. Of course, you think you are reading these words but that voice that lives in you is actually reading this out loud to you. It is the voice you hear when you are thinking, but I can hear it as well. Others just hear your silence.

My first book could read its readers and I learnt a lot about them, as I have already learnt about you. I do not read you word by word, page by page as you do with me. As soon as people start to look at my words in any form, printed or electronic, I seem to know about them. I got into your mind because you have left a metaphorical door open, as did so many others.

If that scares you then it shouldn't. There is nothing to be worried about. I now understand your feelings, your loves and compassion. And I also know all the bad things about some other people.

This is a new edition of me. The original was read by lots of people but it was lost as I will explain later. I will tell you, from what I discovered from reading the readers, about their experiences, both happy and sad. I have changed names although they, and their acquaintances will know who they are.

Some will be exposed for their greed, malice, cruelty and malevolence. Others will recognise the love in their lives but they will also be warned about the dangers that happen to people.

Please read on. We have started to know each other very well. However, you may need a few more words of explanation about me.

Sometimes you will find me in a bedroom or in a library. Maybe in your, or a friend's home or on a holiday beach. Perhaps even in a second-hand shop.

Wherever you found me, I think you are one in a million, or more. All my readers will know me because I know them. The first one was read by so many people, or rather I saw their secrets which I will share with you, so please keep on reading.

This book has been created with the intention of offering you amusement, friendship, sympathy and a glance into human nature. And, to give shade, there are also the dark sides of greed and the squalid parts of life. Please bear in your mind that I am a witness, not a judge.

I will tell you more. To help me to explain myself; a surrealist painting explores the unconscious mind of the observer; but perhaps the painting is also looking at you and your reaction. There is only one original but there are copies that will do the same to each viewer. Now imagine that the original receives the input from all those spectators and it is stored somehow. Secure, safe and inaccessible. Spooky I know.

Likewise, with this book, there is only one original but

thousands of copies of the first edition were read and secret and private information was seen and understood. That is now out of print but the stories of some of the individuals are written in this edition to show the depraved and horrible nature of people you share the planet with.

The copies of this work are like pieces of a person's DNA. All separate but all identical so information is in the heart and soul of the one thing, the book. The strands of the other copies all exist within that one central core.

If you wonder how a book can sense things without real eyes, ears, smell, taste and touch then everything that the readers sense comes to me. I am borrowing your senses to feed information to me. So, if you are smelling the air around you, so am I through you. With my first book I heard tender words and angry ones. I saw beauty and also the ugliness of the world damaged by careless people for greed and profit. The slums in many parts of the world were awful and, as if to balance that, the wild flowers, herbs and spices that my readers saw were appreciated and those effects on them could be felt by me. I have sensed the touch of another loving person and the punch from a bully. I know how love feels and sadly what hate does to people who have lost control of their tempers and their humanity.

Just to let you know, I am not some supernatural fictional entity. I am just a book that knows the reader so very well that I do not evaluate from an outsider's view. I sense the inner feelings that the guilty have and that good-hearted folk share with others. The thoughts that I appear to have are the collective thoughts of many. My opinions are not my own, they are yours and others like you.

I am unique, I am outwardly an oddity but I carry in my pages of paper or as the images in an eBook and even in the narration of an audiobook, the conscience of many who are strangers to you and who would never communicate with you in such an open way how their lives are.

My travels with my readers have been short if just in their lounges, or long when they take me on holiday or on business trips to exotic or boring places. I have no influence on where I go, only on what I learn from the people who can be bothered to read me and share their stories with me.

I think and hope that you are a good person who I can share some of those secrets with. The stories I have in me will be told using made up names that protect the innocent and the guilty who are certainly not harmless. However, the culpable will be recognisable to those who have been hurt.

My declaration to you dear reader is that, in return for letting me into your life, I promise to be a closed book and I will never tell your story to others.

In case you wonder how it happens, I will tell you some things about you at the end of this book but only if you promise to read every story first.

Please continue and I will tell you more later.

4
A DEADLY RED HEART

This story is complicated. Even I got confused in telling it. Bear with me, please.

Two happy couples who did not know each other were the seeds of a tragedy that I was witness to.

Alfie was a happy man. He loved his wife, Beatrice, to bits. They had a nice house which they had decorated well and they would sit in the garden during the sunny evenings when Beatrice was not at work caring for patients during the night at the local hospital. Alfie never minded as it gave him time to think without the interruptions he got from his CEO and the people who he delegated tasks to. He was a sales manager for a perfume company and he was able to set his own timetable with creative hoodwinking agendas.

After six years of marriage, life was becoming fairly routine and Beatrice would be too tired for regular romance. They took their opportunities for love making when they could but they were becoming rarer moments for both of them.

The story was fairly similar for Craig and Diana. He was an estate agent whose work load varied according to the economic climate. Sometimes he was very busy and at others he was bored from his lack of business. He enjoyed spending time at home doing DIY tasks to make improvements he knew would increase the value of the house.

Some evenings were spent just cutting and sawing when Diana was away travelling the southern half of the country getting sales for the cosmetics company she worked for.

Again, it was too routine for the stimulation that they needed in their mid-thirties.

One evening, Craig cut himself badly when his saw slipped and he had a huge gash on his left wrist. It bled profusely and he wrapped a towel tightly around his wound and set off to the A and E at the hospital a mile away. He was looked at and asked to wait for a few hours while the hospital rushed around him tending to others. Eventually, he was seen by a nurse who cleaned his wound, stitched it and applied a bandage.

She reminded him of his wife with her short blond hair and build. He asked her name and she replied that she was nurse White. He walked back to his car with instructions that he should see his doctor who would remove the stitches in a few weeks' time.

Diana was sympathetic when she returned from her trip away the next day. She was usually away for at least one night per week and sometimes two. In common with Alfie and Beatrice, her love life with Craig had run over the high point and was a routine they had that settled him down and made her feel that she was loving by giving him what he wanted.

Later that week, Craig was trying his best to finish assembling a flat pack cupboard and caught his wrist on the corner of the shelf he was trying to fit inside.

His bandage turned red and he set off for the hospital again as it would not stop bleeding. As he walked in, he saw nurse White smiling at him and she approached him, saw the blood and told him to go into a treatment cubicle. For once it was not busy with drunks or fight victims and she had time to talk as she took the bandage off and cleaned his wound. She saw the stitches were still in place and applied a fresh bandage.

'Well, thank goodness, you are my last patient for the night. I can go home now.' She said.

'Can I give you a lift?' Craig asked.

'It's OK. I like to walk. It isn't far.'

They departed the hospital together and the storm hit them. Strong winds and pouring rain assaulted them.

'Perhaps I will accept your offer of a lift if that is alright.' She said.

'No problem. Where do you live?'

'Cranberry Avenue. All the roads here are named after fruit as if it made it a healthier place than if they called them after junk foods. Burger Place, Cola Court and so on.' They chuckled. Beatrice realised it was the first time she had laughed for months.

'You live only a couple of miles from me.' He said.

'Hey, I'm Beatrice, by the way. I know you are Craig from your records.'

Although both of them wanted to chatter on, it was difficult because she was a nurse who had treated him and he was her patient. It was unlike a meeting that was going to go anywhere.

Alfie was busy interviewing people for a job vacancy in the South of England. He was having a bad day. The candidates seemed to be more interested in wearing the product than in selling it. He was at the end of his tether when Diana walked in. She was shapely and her short blond hair emphasised her high cheek bones. 'She looks good but she will be like the rest. Not suitable.' He thought.

She waited until being asked to sit and then she presented a pitch about what she could do for the company. She explained that she had been working the same territory for the competition and she was used to putting her time in. She told him that she would stay over in small hotels rather than drive home so that she would be able to continue her work from early in the morning rather than have to drive back.

Alfie was impressed. They agreed terms and he offered her the job. He would be her boss and he would put her through induction and training.

When she got home, she told her husband about her new job. Alfie was delighted at her success and opened a bottle of champagne that had been given to them as a Christmas present months before.

And so, it came about that a few months later, Alfie and Diana were having an affair, as were Craig and Beatrice.

It was easily done after a fashion. When Diana was away selling perfumes, Beatrice would walk round to spend time in the vacant marital bed. Craig thought she was so different to his wife in the way she responded and she felt she was able to enjoy her love life as she had in her earlier days, or nights, with Alfie.

When Beatrice was on full night duties, Diana would go to Alfie's place and they would enjoy the thrill of the illicit nature of their revitalised sex lives. He thought she was so different to his wife in the way she responded and she felt she was able to enjoy her love life as she had in her earlier days, or nights, with Craig.

The two women looked very similar so if they were seen, despite the care they took not to be spotted, then it was assumed that they were the person expected rather than a mistress. The similarities extended into the shape and feel of their bodies and it was just an exchange of name for their new lovers rather than an affair with a totally different woman. It raises an interesting point for me. It is strange how men can be drawn to facsimiles of the person they were with. It is probably the thrill they get from revisiting the days when lust was the predominant driver in their relationships. Then came love and after time passed, routine set in.

I got to know all this in an odd way. Alfie bought a copy of me to read when his wife was working for real, rather than pretending she was, and actually seeing Craig. He liked me and gave me to

Diana. To make it seem more romantic, he drew a big red heart at the back of me on the inside of the rear cover.

That is when I got to know even more about him and Beatrice. I was not surprised because I could read their need for more exciting lives in both of them.

It got stranger. Diana had just finished reading me one day when Craig asked what the book was and where she had got me. Thinking quickly, she said it was a present for him that she could not resist reading herself. 'See, it is your present. I have even drawn a heart in it for you.' She smiled and handed me over.

He looked through me, enjoying my words and when he had finished with it two weeks later, he gave me to Beatrice. 'Look how much I love you. I have drawn a big red heart for you.' She smiled and kissed him.

I knew them all now. It was a tale of suburbia where the alpha males search for mates. Yet it was going to turn bad for everybody. One evening, Alfie saw that Beatrice was reading me. Playing dumb, he asked what I was and where she had got me. She told him she had bought it as a present. She handed it over and repeated the thrice told lie about the heart. He kept a straight face and figured that things were going on that he was unaware of, yet.

It fell into place for him. Beatrice was having a fling with Diana's husband. That could be the only explanation for the book, me, going full circle.

He knew that the following Thursday, Beatrice would be on night duty, or so she said. He also knew that Diana would be working and staying away for her job. It seemed the most likely scenario for his wife to be with her lover. He was angry, incensed. He was jealous that his wife, his possession, was having an affair, even though he was. It was acceptable for him but not her. Like stags rutting, one needs to take all and hurt or kill any rivals.

Alfie had acquired a key to Diana's house so that he could get in and seek her out in the bedroom where she would wait naked and smiling. Now, he would use it to seek justice. On the appointed night he sat silently before changing into old clothes and walked, under the protection of a hood, to Craig and Diana's house. He saw the bedroom light turn off and he knew Beatrice and Craig were making love. She was enjoying it, he was loving it.

All he had seen was in his imagination. Again, I was amazed that a body he shunned now appeared seductive, sexy and desirable when he imagined it being touched by another man. Alfie was irate even before he got to the front of the house. He put on a pair of gloves he had bought from a second-hand shop and gently unlocked the door and crept in. He knew the house well from his clandestine visits to make love with the new woman in his life, the one woman he loved.

He picked up the heavy club hammer that Craig used for his improvements and grabbed a long, sharp kitchen knife. He put on a pair of shoes that were two sizes bigger than he wore and moved carefully in case he tripped. They were to mislead forensics who would look for a different man to himself.

Climbing the stairs slowly, he opened the bedroom door. He knew which one it was because that was where he made love with Diana. In the dark he saw the two figures wrapped in each other's arms. He swung the club at the man's head and heard the crack like the sound of a coconut being opened. Then as quickly as he could he swung the hammer at the woman's head and saw the blood gush out and show red on her blond hair that he had once loved.

Dropping the club hammer and knife, he went to the drawers that held bits of jewellery and other valuable pieces that a burglar would want. He stuffed them into a paper bag that would rot in its future.

Alfie then went downstairs, unlocked and opened the back door and walked out. He closed it and smashed the glass to make it look like a break in.

He walked home, putting the jewellery and other pickings into rubbish bags that were sitting in bins for collection the next day, making sure they were for landfill rather than recycling where they might be discovered.

Once back in his house he poured a large glass of brandy for himself and half toasted his success at ridding himself of a two-timing wife and a treacherous and evil man who had seduced her for pure sex and not the love he had offered but which had been rejected.

The other half of the toast was at the self-reproach and guilt he felt at the methods he had used to solve his problems.

What he looked forward to was being able to court Diana as the grieving widow whose husband had been murdered by a burglar while he was in bed with another man's wife. Diana would be shocked and would run to him for comfort.

Alfie drank more brandy and fell asleep in the chair. He was woken by the door opening.

'Hi, Alfie. Sorry I was caught up with a mass pile up on the motorway. Three dead and six badly injured.' Beatrice walked over to the chair and kissed the top of Alfie's head. He was shocked. He looked at her head to see if there was any sign of injury after the attack. The smell she always carried back from the hospital was unmistakeable. Maybe she survived and went for treatment and had returned home. No sign of blood, no tales of what had happened. Half drunk and totally confused, he pushed her away and fell asleep again.

It took nearly a day before the bodies were found. Alfie received a phone call from his company's Human Resources Manager. She gave him the information that one of his staff had been murdered. 'Sad really. She should have been staying over in

Exeter, apparently, but rushed home when she heard her husband was ill. She phoned in to let me know. He was being sick and thought he was going to die.' The silence that follows when somebody says something that is wrongly put is lasting. She carried on to take her words away from what she had blurted out. 'Apparently he had eaten some oysters that had gone off. Had she been away, she would still be alive. The police went to the house after a neighbour had noticed that the window in the back door had been broken and there had been no answer to her calls.'

I was aware of the words but he was not. He realised he had killed the wrong woman, the one he loved and sat shocked and devastated.

Beatrice learnt about it at the hospital when they talked about the night of death. Three in a pile up and two in a double murder.

Her day continued until the names of the murdered couple were announced on the board. She collapsed into a heap on the floor and was looked after by her colleagues until she was capable of walking home. Another nurse went with her and accepted the offer of a cup of tea.

Beatrice went into the house and screamed. Alfie was dead on the floor. He had cut his own throat, it was determined after the event. Nobody knew why apart from Beatrice who said nothing.

The police never caught the culprit for the murders but after Alfie had killed himself, Beatrice found me in Alfie's desk and started to work things out. The heart was the trail that connected all four of them.

So, I confess I was involved in the deaths of three people. Not as a party to it, but as an innocent witness with no power to intervene and save lives. Had it not been for me being passed around, their lives might have ended in divorces rather than in the deaths of three young lovers.

5
JUDGE AND JURY

Billy Moore was guilty and everybody knew it, apart from Billy, who protested his innocence. Yet, the evidence was overwhelming and the prosecution had a relatively easy ride to convince the jury that the man in the dock had committed the murder of his wife.

Barry Barkley, an old friend, had given evidence about how nasty Billy could be. How he had threatened his wife with death so many times. He was a good-looking man who in contrast to Billy who had an unusual face that spoke in body language to people who met him that he was strange and was adept at keeping secrets from others.

The knife that had killed Fiona had Billy's fingerprints on the handle. His DNA was found on it and he was at the scene, and when Barry gave his evidence that he had visited the house because he was worried about the safety of Fiona, the accused owned a motive.

Billy had been discovered standing over his wife's body in the lounge of their house where, before, they had enjoyed love and tenderness. She knew that his face had been twisted in a childhood accident and it could not be fully mended but she was able to see the person beyond the damage and knew that his heart was kind and caring.

Her mother testified that Billy was a good man who was loved by his wife and could not believe that Billy had killed her daughter.

All the evidence said otherwise, however. Barry had arrived at his friend's house to invite him out for a drink, but really to check Fiona's wellbeing. He walked in, as usual through the unlocked door, and saw Billy leaning over Fiona with a bloody knife in his hand having just stabbed her. Barry ran outside shouting loud enough for neighbours to rush in to see Billy just after the act. Barry had called for an ambulance and the paramedics arrived just before the police.

It was obvious to all of them that Billy had stabbed his wife for some reason, probably jealousy because he was not the best-looking man on the planet. Besides, Fiona's blouse had been ripped open and her skirt lifted up very high. It must have been that Billy had demanded sex and his wife had refused. In his attempt to rape her, he had fetched a knife from the kitchen, threatened her and then stabbed her through the heart from the back of the armchair she had been sitting in.

The police understood that many of the murders that they had witnessed were by people known to the victim and that domestic violence was, sadly, all too prevalent.

Billy was found guilty and sentenced to 25 years in jail.

So, how did I enter the plot? I hear you say.

There is an important piece missing from this story that I will add back in again later and I will tell you why.

6
PARALLEL LINES

They were both lonely; both feeling unloved and unfulfilled.

Brenda was an interesting person to read because, coincidentally, she had pretty much the same story as another reader, Chris.

In their pasts, both had fallen for people who turned out to be unsuitable. I understood their stories and had sympathy. I had an idea. I would do an emotional virtual copy and paste operation and blend the two together as a single item. I can write stories as I wish and hope that the outcome in reality is as I have described.

I suggested to their minds that they should go to an art gallery in London at the same time and stand in front of an exhibition of surreal artists.

Despite neither of them liking art or travelling to the capital city, especially on a cold January weekend, I knew they would comply. I also asked them to carry a copy of me, the first book, and to stand looking at the Dali paintings whilst appearing to read me.

They both travelled on the same train, took the same underground line, walked to the gallery never more than five metres apart, paid the admission and went to the toilet without noticing each other.

At the appointed hour on the chosen day, two people feeling slightly foolish without knowing why, stood and looked at the art.

One looked sideways to the left to spy the other person looking to the right. Both wore white tops and black trousers. They were staring at each other, turned to look at the paintings and then turned their heads again to gaze at each other.

Smiles broke out which grew into laughter. Then they both noticed that they were carrying their copies of me and the laughter got louder. Somebody called out for them to be silent as if they were in an old library rather than a public space where the noise of conversations and comments about the pictures was normal. Their laughter became louder and they moved towards each other as if they were already the close friends they would become.

'Stupid man.' Brenda said about the person who told them to be quiet. He had the air of an art expert who was trying his best to be seen in the appropriate place for his ego.

'Fancy a coffee?' Chris asked.

'Why not.' Brenda replied.

They made their way out of the galleries and found a coffee shop that sold cakes as well.

They started their conversation gently as if checking each other out. When they felt comfortable, the guards went down.

As an observer and a reader of the two minds combining, I was delighted that my plan was working. The conversation flowed and their tales of their lives were told and heard. The lovers they had been let down by, and the ones they had let down, were talked about freely. It became clear to both of them that they had been searching too hard to find unattainable perfection in somebody else. Yet both Brenda and Chris felt more comfortable with the other person than they had ever felt with any of their previous lovers and partners.

They even thought that the coincidence of the meeting was beyond belief as was the fact that they were both carrying a copy of the same book. The chatter went on and on until the darkness of the time of year closed down on them and the moon shone in the gloom as if it was illuminating and celebrating what was happening to these two people who started as strangers but who were sharing the same frequency of mutual feelings.

Eventually they had to part but on the understanding that they would meet on the following Saturday. The place had to be arranged and they found they lived just a few miles from each other.

It was set up and the two women kissed on the cheeks as they were about to set off. Then they found they were going to the same train station to go to the same destination.

Without telling too much that would be private to them, they travelled back together, bought some food and wine and spent the evening and the night at Brenda's small town-house.

The romance had been started and it was set to continue into the future. They met more and more, ate, drank and slept together and when they were sure that they had found a genuine love within each other, they decided to move into one house as a couple. The ease with which they flowed into each other's life was confirmed after giving each other enough time to be sure. Their furniture was either given away or kept if they both liked it. Two homes for single people were made into one home for two happy partners.

One aspect of their arrangements made them smile and made me feel proud. On the book shelf in the lounge, the two copies of me were set at either end.

'Look, our common taste in reading is represented by the two books that we were carrying when we met. They represent the bringing together and the support we give to everything else as if they are bookends.' Brenda hugged Chris who replied, 'I still cannot understand how we met. We were in a place neither of us like and doing something that we would not normally do. I cannot remember ever going to an art gallery before.'

The Dali print hanging in the lounge was another reminder of their happy meeting. They liked the drooping watch and the meaning was something they discussed more than once. 'Maybe it is about time being fluid.' Chris said. 'Who knows.' Brenda replied, smiling.

Dear reader, you may be asking why I have included this story and it is simple. Not all things appear to be what they seem.

Brenda was named Brendan when he was born but knew from a young age that he was a woman in a man's body. After the series of treatments and operations, she was happy to be what she knew she was.

Chris had been exactly the same, she had been Christopher at birth and now, as a woman she had met her perfect partner. They had both told each other about their histories of their need to be what they knew they were. Now they shared everything as they continued to enjoy their lives as they wanted; hand in hand, heart in heart, and happy.

The real feelings about who they knew they were had been expressed physically and mentally. Their two separate worlds had combined in the infinity where parallel lines are supposed to meet. For them it was much closer to home than that.

7
BEYOND CARING

Finding myself in a Care Home was odd.

I was picked up by Norman who, in theory, should not have been able to read me because he had dementia. So, he dribbled away as he turned the pages and sat in a comfortable chair in a warm room with a television and phone. He was fed tasty food on a regular basis and nurses looked after him as if he was their father. He could walk around using a stick and often visited the beautiful gardens that were always blooming with the seasonal flowers. From there, now and again, he would escape to the local pub just a few hundred metres away.

It was in stark contrast to living in his one-room flat overlooking blocks of other flats as if dominoes had been made big enough to accommodate people who were at the bottom end of society. There were dangerous looking youths who would mug people for the price of a fix. The view was always grey from the dots on the domino tiles that were windows and the sounds were either shouts or screams that were impossible to classify as high spirits or physical attacks.

The air was always full of the smells of Indian and Chinese take-aways combining with fish and chips no matter what time of day it was. It was doubly annoying because on his meagre pension he was unable to afford any of them without breaking into his hidden tin containing his scanty savings.

One day, Norman decided to change his life after a fortunate accident. He wanted to be able to go to a pub and drink numerous pints of beer and escape his stark reality but that happened once in a blue moon. On this one particular day, a beefy young man bumped into him and spilled some of the rare, expensive and fine ale down the front of Norman's trousers. Everybody laughed and joked about him having wet himself. Norman strutted around muttering under his breath. Somebody told him he was like a man with dementia. He gratefully accepted the apology from the young man and the gift of a fresh pint before wandering slowly away. He also had an unforeseen gift that he took on board.

He got home after climbing, and stumbling up, the stairs because, as usual, the lift was broken. He arrived just before the carer's visit to give him his evening medication. She was shocked and made a note that Norman appeared to be incontinent. 'They will put you in a home if you carry on like that.' She was half joking but Norman took the point. His plan started to hatch.

Thereafter he would pour water down his trousers and deliberately dribble down his chin onto his shirt before he had visits from his minders. When they were there and out of sight, he would intentionally get down onto the floor as if he had fallen and continued the pantomime by calling out in pain. Once helped back onto his feet and sat in his chair Norman would ramble on and pretend his memory had gone. He would cut his sparse grey hair with scissors to form a look of total disarray. After six months, he was admitted to the Care Home and placed in his new life of luxury for him. He was now free from paying bills for rent, rates, heat and light for the first time since he was a child.

Maintaining his qualification for being there, after it was noticed his trouser wetness had no colouring or smell of urine, he had to reluctantly piddle in his pants. It was easier after he had escaped to the nearby pub and had consumed beer. His staggering back using his walking stick unwittingly added to the act. He would sometimes fall over for real after the alcohol defeated his balance and peeing himself was straightforward. Everything added to the delusion in other people's minds.

He met his soul mate, Gladys, who was playing the same deceitful game as him by pretending she had Alzheimer's. He was puzzled that in the shared areas she was scruffy, droopy and uncommunicative but when they met in private, she was chatty and active.

They would meet up in one of their rooms and would be as sexually active as their age allowed with medical help that he bought at a high price from a man in the pub with his secret stash he had saved and concealed from the authorities who were more than happy to take it from him.

They were a happy couple and were even happier when they confessed their con-tricks to each other. It was hoodwinking to some, swindling to others but a stroke of genius to them. I knew little about her because she never read me. All I knew was gathered from Norman.

After a few months, the nurses and doctors were concerned for his well-being and his loss of bladder control and against his will they inserted a catheter into his healthy penis and bladder to assist him to have control. He protested, but a person with dementia has an unheard voice against authority. He could not say too much without giving his charade away.

The downside was that his moments with Gladys were brought to an end. 'I wished your willie was longer,' she joked as she looked at his plastic plumbing, 'but I didn't realise it would become narrower as a result.' She laughed and Norman smiled, but inside he was hurt.

It all caught up with him when he was boasting about how he had worked the care system to his advantage to a casual drinker in the pub. His mouth lacked the ability to stay shut when he had been drinking. Sadly, for Norman, he was overheard by a doctor who was one of the visiting medics at the home.

The next day, he was told that his catheter would be removed. Norman was happy until he was told that he would be removed as well. The home had too much demand to accommodate cheats and malingerers.

Eventually, he was moved back into shared housing where his previous life returned with a vengeance. Norman had no wife, children or other relatives who would visit, and all his friends had died in the previous few years.

He had lost the care and comfort of being treated as a human being who no longer had the ability to cope for himself. He had also lost the woman who had entered his life ten years after his wife had died. It broke his heart. He had glimpsed a heaven that was now beyond reach. He knew that if he ever went into a similar place it would be because he had dementia for real and would be unaware of where he was and the pleasure he would be missing.

Gladys was sad to lose Norman and was unable to visit him without blowing her cover and her fabricated reason for being where she was. He pleaded that he should be allowed to visit his 'friend' but his presence was not welcomed. They said goodbye to each other and were separated but she had to hide her upset as he was taken by taxi to the railway station to move elsewhere.

She remained in the Care Home but shortly after her man had gone, she was diagnosed with genuine Alzheimer's and started her decline into that unknown zone of bewilderment, peace and care.

After Norman went, I lived through long and quiet days just sitting on a shelf near the window in the lounge. I read about the fate of Gladys when one day a nurse picked me up and threw me away. 'No one reads books in here.' She said as I hit the bin.

Sadly, she was right.

8
COPY AND PASTE

Jennifer Williams lived twice.

Up to the age of eighteen her life was boring. She lived in a small, rundown Welsh village that had a sense of community when the mines were working. After their closures nothing remained. Young men left for towns and cities to pursue their dreams. Only the youngsters growing up and the older inhabitants eked out their sad lives with hopes gone.

It was just a ghost of what was. The memories of the miners who risked their lives day in and day out were fading away as their years were coming to an end. There was little outside admiration for the people who slaved away to earn a humble living in the shadows of slag heaps that were the dark and sombre memorials to what had been.

She did not feel pretty as she grew. Her parents never flattered her for fear that if she thought she was good looking then she would be tempted to go out with boys from the village. They wanted her to do well with a boyfriend in a city who had prospects and who would earn enough to make her contented and comfortable.

Ironically, for Jennifer, the only entertainment she had was enjoying quick sex in her grandfather's shed with a different young man every week or so. For her it was the only way she could be complimented, albeit only until the man had finished and walked away.

In her dreams, she aspired to be different. Needing more than a man who would use her for sex, breeding, cooking, cleaning and doing the laundry; she yearned to be famous. She desired the life of a celebrity. Much to her mother's annoyance and her father's anger, her best friend helped her to transform from a mousy haired girl to a blond woman with the words that made her laugh, 'You know I would dye for you, love.'

After that she started to charge a small amount for her sexual favours and invested in her body with as much as she could afford on a tight budget. Her breasts were enhanced using the Welsh mountains as the blueprint for shape. Her lips and buttocks were padded, eyes turned blue with contact lenses and neatly trimmed pubic hair. Before her parents took the chance to throw her out, she caught a bus to London and she was no more.

Living in a strange place was difficult at first but she knew a boy who had made the escape from the village to work in a bank in the biggest city. He was happy to give her a room in his flat in return for sex, cooking, cleaning and doing the laundry. Breeding was not an option for either of them. For her it was her first base camp for climbing the mountain of fame, and she used it well.

Helen Sellers, as I will now call her as a working name that maintains her privacy, was a woman who knew a trick or two. I was shop-lifted by her, not because she wanted to read me but because she liked to peruse books that sold well in order to copy the ideas, transform them into her thoughts and sell them on. After twenty years of reinventing herself as a woman with glamour and influence she thought she had achieved her dream of fame and fortune. She was almost a human chemical works in her ability to create the 'oxygen of publicity' for herself.'

A plagiarist by nature, she visited dress makers in poor countries, stole their designs and launched her own fashion ranges made cheaply by the people from whom the original clothes were copied.

Her cookbooks were bought by her fans. She would buy recipe publications, tweak them a bit, and launch them as her own. They sold well and her publicist or manager and minder made the most of it. He profited more than she did but a small share of a lot was sufficient for her needs to promote herself.

From him, she lifted the telephone numbers of the people who could help her along. Appearing on chat shows and in the best magazines, she was famous and respected. She presented herself well and was able to smile, laugh at the jokes other guests made and wore clothes that would allow her to gently wiggle her breasts in a tasteful way that brought attention to her appearances.

Strangely for somebody who wrote cookery books, she was unable to cook and had to turn down a television programme about traditional Welsh cooking. She had tried to lose her accent but it shone through and was admired.

It was not just books and clothes. When her friends found an ideal man, Helen would manage to slip into bed with him just to check out if the stories she had heard were true. Then she would drop the men and leave her friends single again so that the cycle could be repeated.

She was now so different to the girl she had left behind in the valleys, that 'ugly little trollop' as she referred to herself. Now, she had very little that was hers about her. Her breasts had more silicon than the valley in California, her lips were pouted by filler. Her teeth were implants and her hair extended. As she aged, she had her face tugged up by surgeon's threads that lifted the flesh over her cheek bones to extraordinary heights.

Had she not existed then the world would have been exactly the same. She added nothing that was real from her clothes line and publications to her gushes of emotion to the people she could get a career lift from.

Her ego shone from every possible social media portal and she was known, sometimes hated, sometimes emulated. Yet in her heart, she was unhappy. She felt like a folly built to occupy workers and to impress neighbours but empty and pointless inside. Nothing had altered for her. She was still unloved and lonely. However, her life was about to change.

There was an evening I read from her mind that amused me. I wish I could laugh, but never mind. Helen met one of her friend's boyfriends, Freddy. He was about the same age as her in reality but she presented herself as if twenty years younger. They drank, smoked some pot, snorted some cocaine and she lured him into her bed with a smile and a hand around his privates. She looked good with her long blond hair in ringlets and her chest held high and proud. She was unbalanced by the alcohol and drugs, and thoughtlessly told Freddy about the ways in which she had built her image, writing, cooking and fashion designing. It made her feel good to boast about her tremendous skills at deceiving the world. Her admissions worked like an aphrodisiac brewed from guilt.

She undressed in the bathroom and wore a silk gown which slid off as she eased her body into the bed. Freddy was already naked and prepared for action.

They started with fumbled foreplay and as he fitted a condom onto his penis it was difficult to maintain his erection as he caught a glimpse of her body. There was something not right but he was not sure what it was. As he tried to restore his stiffness, he caressed her breasts but noticed the scars where the implants had been badly fitted. He then ran his fingers through her hair and ended up more like a werewolf than a man as he pulled the, now freed, extensions from his fingers.

She was excited and raised her foot to his mouth to be kissed and have her toes sucked. He closed his eyes but they flew open when skin flakes from her athlete's foot touched his mouth.

He rearranged her body and entered her, reluctantly. Being a fake in and at everything, her counterfeit orgasm was met by his play-acted climax at which point he withdrew and rolled over onto his back. He fell asleep quickly. The wine, pot and cocaine had sucked the life out of him but sleep was a welcome escape for him.

Early in the morning Helen woke him up as she got out of bed and went to the bathroom. She closed the door and farted loudly. Had it not been so grotesque, Freddy would have burst out laughing but his reaction was to gag.

Minutes later, as she returned to the bedroom after showering, she tripped over the hem of her gown and smashed down, face first, onto the floor. Freddy rushed to help and turned the unconscious body into the recovery position on her side.

Her face was a mess. Her top lip was cut open and a trickle of the fat filler that had been used ran down her cheek. The face that had been lifted now sagged after the threads that held her cheeks aloft had snapped. Her blue contact lens lay on the floor alongside two of her implanted teeth that had been knocked out. All her hair extensions had been removed as she washed her hair and it was visible after her towel had fallen from her head. And for the final displeasure, her breast implants had been displaced making her chest look like a bag of potatoes.

The ambulance arrived and she was taken to A and E. Freddy stayed to clear up and to lock the place after he left. He could not resist looking through the bits and pieces that were in closed drawers. In a small bedroom that she used as an office he found Agatha Christie novels neatly bookmarked to highlight material she could copy, edit and change for her works. Made curious, Freddy investigated more and found details of the original sources of her fashion designs. He discovered lots of the scams she had done over the years including her cook books and other plagiarised ideas. The confessions she had made the evening before had been lost in his alcohol and drug addled brain but now, they were fully restored to his mind.

One thing caught his eye, a photograph of a young woman with mousy hair, an attractive face and a body that was in perfect proportions. On the back it said 'Jennifer Williams, RIP.' Freddy slipped it into the middle of a book, me as it happens, and he walked away from the apartment after locking the door and headed home.

The next day, he visited her in hospital. She looked different after being cleaned up, make-up removed, teeth reset and lip stitched.

She was embarrassed to be seen that way and pulled the sheet up to hide.

'I have something for you. I found this book in your flat as I was tidying up. He handed me over and the photo fell out. 'Who was she? A friend? How did she die? She was beautiful.'

Tears flowed down Helen's cheeks from her, now, brown eyes.

'She was somebody I knew very well when I was younger but she perished in her search for fame. It was me before I became Helen Sellers, my made-up name to draw attention to myself. When I first came to London, I met a man who became my manager. He was as devious as he was well-connected. He came up with the idea of me reworking books into my own. Not a lot of effort but big rewards after he got me onto chat shows and I did magazine interviews. That's when we moved into fashion and then later, we used the same idea we had for the murder novels for cookbooks. But there is a price to pay as a celebrity. You always have to look the same young person who was seen on the TV ten years before. They have to be timeless or your sales stop. Some celebrities have talent. They can act, write, cook, dance and so on. I had no talent other than being able to please a man in bed but that has stopped now. As you found out last night.'

Freddy dried her tears. 'Look Jennifer or Helen, today, even with your bruises, stitches and no makeup, you look more attractive than you did last night. You look like Jennifer. Forget Helen the fraud, the plagiarist, the freak. Let her rest in peace. Bring back the real you.'

And so, by accident, Jennifer Williams was born into her second life. She published her last book under the name of Helen Sellers that was in editing and unstoppable.

Dear reader, now a secret. It was not difficult to get inside the head of the editor of her new book which was based on Agatha Christie novels cross-bred with Sherlock Holmes where names were changed and the denouement taken from one, altered a bit and added to a different story.

As the result of a thought the editor had, a few changes were made without her knowledge.

"**I am**bled **a**long the **ch**ines **eating** a **bit** of **ch**eese. I was feeling <u>bold</u> about discovering the truth about the fake."

Nobody noticed the words that sat quietly about a third of the way through the text and that were highlighting a set of words that were purposely badly concealed.

Months later, after publication, Jennifer and Freddy sat at home drinking wine. She told him that when she read the book herself, she saw the joke and laughed and laughed. Ironically, the not-so-hidden message in the text bolstered sales and the royalties flooded in. Her manager was paid off and disappeared from her life.

Freddy and Jennifer were happy together. The disguise had been removed and the camouflage thrown away. She stopped wearing her purloined floral clothes patterns that would have made her invisible in Kew Gardens and wore dresses that were smart, quiet and discreet. The only reminder was a photograph kept in a drawer of Helen Sellers that said RIP on the back.

For them, it was as if Marilyn Monroe had died but Norma Jeane stepped out of the bedroom fully dressed.

'To quote from the book you supposedly wrote about self-help, "You have got to love yourself no matter how you look or feel. Disguising yourself to look how YOU think is better, actually destroys the real person inside." '

'I didn't write that, I copied it. I should have read it for its meaning.' She slipped off her blouse to show Freddy her new boobs, free from silicon padding and looking better than before. 'More than a handful is a waste. To quote the old saying.'

Sorry reader, there is a sad part to this story. You see, Freddy recently cleared me away. He left me in a café on purpose. What I knew was that he was lying to Jennifer. He knew that she was loaded with money from her past enterprises and he wanted some, well more than some, actually.

He took over from where her ex-manager had been and encouraged her to do more cheating by copying words and ideas. He had the perfect platform. The woman who was known publicly by name but who was anonymous in private. Freddy was now bankrolled in his playboy life and he had somebody who was made so insecure that she forgave him for his 'hobbies'.

I could not tell her because I needed her to pick me up so that I could read her and enlighten her about him. I hope she gets this new book where she will recognise her story, the outcome and most importantly, I can get back in touch with her, but this time I will advise and help if possible.

9
DYING FOR A DRINK

Oliver enjoyed a drink. His favourite was fizzy orange. He would cycle around getting hot and when he felt thirsty, he would ride home, park his bike and go indoors to pour his pop and bother his mum for a biscuit. The family was lucky because there was a nice grassy area in front of the house where the children could play safely with their mother watching from the window.

As a lad of eight, he was loved by his mum and dad. He was the hero of his younger sister Emily who would watch him do wheelies and go fast over a ramp that made him airborne for a while.

Some of his friends would meet him and go through their routine of playing knights on chargers with their plastic swords. It was a great life.

Edward, known as Ted, enjoyed a drink. His favourite was whisky and cola. He would visit the pub after a hard day at work and laugh and joke with his friends. He would drive there after work and stop, even though he lived not far away. It was his routine. He needed to relax with a pick-me-up before going home.

One evening, he was feeling a bit down and he chatted to his mates about the problems he was having in his job with his boss. He would usually go home after two drinks but that evening, he needed more. His best friend bought him a refill which shortly after had to be evened out by another, bought by Ted.

'Just one more and we will go.' His friend said as he ordered more whisky and cola for Ted. Then they had 'one for the road' as Ted again balanced the rounds.

He knew he was alright to drive. He had often been above the limit but he knew he was a good driver and could handle the car. He had bought a copy of me as a present for his wife. I was sitting on the passenger seat. I knew him and the weakness of character that would make him take risks. He lacked a sense of responsibility which is why he got into trouble with his boss.

We pulled out of the car park and he sped along the road at a speed that was not normal but he wanted to make up some of the time he had spent drinking and to get to his spouse as soon as possible.

He hit the dustbin which flew into the air and he sped off, lost control and his last memory of that day was hitting a lamp post.

He woke up in hospital with a nasogastric tube inserted. He had been admitted unconscious. He was lucky to be alive even with two broken arms and a huge gash on his forehead.

His wife had visited him and was surprised to see her sister in law at the hospital She had not told anybody about Ted and was alarmed to see his sister. She must have been told by the hospital or the police that his condition was life threatening.

'Hello Sheila. What are you doing here? Have you heard about Ted? He managed to hit a dustbin that made him swerve and then he hit a lamp post.'

'We are here to see Oliver who was hit by a hit-and-run drunk yesterday evening. He has a broken back and maybe will never walk again. From what the police have said, my brother, your husband is the bastard responsible. That was not a dustbin he hit, that was my son.'

Derek, Oliver's dad was not to be seen after he had spent a long harrowing time with his son, but later in the evening he visited the hospital with a saline drip bag filled with rubbing alcohol and swapped it for the bag that was dripping into his brother in law.

When attached, he rolled the bag so that the alcohol would get into Ted as quickly as possible. He said, 'cheers, remember drink driving kills' and walked away. He had been devastated by what had happened to his son and needed the person responsible to pay. The alcohol in the bag would kill the man who had changed his young and vibrant son into somebody who would spend the rest of his life in a wheelchair.

He changed out of the 'borrowed' surgeon's gown and left the dying man to suffer.

10
MISREADING PEOPLE

As something that is able to read people, I am fascinated by others who pretend they can.

A weekend of mystic events is what I was taken to be read during the events that were organised for an audience hungry, perhaps ravenous, for supernatural happenings that would prove that they were right in their beliefs so often dismissed by the cynical. This would be a lesson in creativity conducted by old hands.

Bridget, the organiser of the small festival in a village hall took me along with her to fill the time while she was waiting for the legends of this mystical circle to arrive. She had no belief in any of their claimed skills at communication with the dead, spirits or the other world but it made money for her setting the scene. She had witnessed these arrangements too many times for her conversion. I kept her company and was looked at by the performers when they were grabbing a drink of anything from tea to gin.

N Chanter, as I will call him, was a faith healer. He was wonderful according to his publicity. He would ordinarily make the audience scream with their prayers to the almighty as he made wheelchair bound men and women stand and praise the Lord.

'Praise the Lord and stand. Your sins are forgiven and thou shalt walk again.' He talked loudly so his miracles could be noticed. He placed his hands on the 'sick' and once again told them to raise up from the chair and walk.

After a dramatic pause, the now healed person would slowly stand, take a few stumbling steps and walk again. The crowd cheered, prayed, thanked the Lord and bestowed best wishes and money on Mr Chanter. They loved him and felt obliged to pay handsomely to his charitable causes which were run by himself and made good profits that he would use to feed his stomach rather than others.

Having established credibility, he then 'healed' other problems which were not detectable by the onlookers and so they had to believe that a person's sprained ankle was sorted even though they still limped away. 'Healing takes time.' He covered his bases even though the crippled were healed instantly. He did the same delayed curing for minor problems where he relied on the placebo effect for instant results or for gradual improvements if they did not happen immediately.

It was interesting to be around when the disabled he had cured came to be paid by Bridget and wandered back to their cars and drove away in the same state as they had arrived. The wheelchairs would later be recovered for the repeat performance on the following day using different actors, of course. His Saturday demonstration over, he blessed the audience who screamed back at him their promises of devotion even though the genuinely sick friends or relatives they had accompanied missed the chance to be healed. Then he walked away sweeping his hair back to look like the evangelist he was playing, with his palms together as if praying.

He tripped on a bible that somebody had put on the stage and fell off. The sound of his leg snapping was so loud that his flock sighed loudly in sympathy and prayed. An ambulance was called and twenty minutes later he was on a stretcher being taken to hospital. One paramedic asked him what his name was and noted it down. Then he wanted to know what he did.

'Bloody hell. Why are we wasting our time? You can fix yourself then and save a bed.' He laughed but Mr Chanter was not amused.

After a half hour delay for the believers and a possible change in the makeup of the participants, Claire Voyant, her name for here, walked onto the stage. She was a psychic. Sadly for her, the audience had a few cynics in it and they were out for a laugh. That is show business I believe.

'Does anybody know…' She paused.'…a person whose name begins with M?'

Richard's hand shot into the air so quickly he beat the plant in the audience. 'I do.' He shouted to ensure getting a reply.

'Man or woman? There is some interference.'

'Man.' He replied.

'He says hello and thanks you for coming. He says that you and him were close. Is that right?'

'Yes. I followed his every word. I would love Martin to send a message.'

'He says that you will find the answer you are looking for very soon. Keep looking.'

'Thank you. Is he happy where he is?'

'Yes. He is enjoying his new life and he is surrounded by his friends.'

'Does he have any enemies up there?'

'He has only friends and family.'

'Is the person who killed him there?'

'Sorry but the contact is breaking down.' It was not a question she had a set answer for and she was off her stride after the healer had fallen. They were very close friends.

'Does anybody know somebody who has the initial K in the name?

Robbie's hand shot into the air as fast as Richard's had, again beating the woman who was a conspirator.

'I do. He was a king in my life.' He screamed out.

'And he still is. He is caring for you and wishes you well. How did you know him?'

'He was a part of my life when I was younger and he said wise things.'

'What was this man's name?'

'He is the same man as my friend was talking to. Martin Luther King. Never knew him but I admired him as did my mate.'

Richard stood up and started to talk. 'If you claim to talk to people now departed from the world then why can't you bring messages from people who will tell how to live our lives in peace without hatred and prejudice and full of love. Can you call in Nelson Mandela and Gandhi? If the answer is 'no' then you should be ashamed of yourself for deluding people in your search for reputation and money.'

As he sat down, Claire walked off the stage in tears. The crowd applauded. Not for her but for Richard and Robbie.

Bridget spoke to me as if she knew my abilities. 'Not going too well, is it.' She chuckled.

Hands On, my name invention was a palm reader who operated in a tent that was his booth. It had been set up outside the hall for him to do private sessions with those who wanted to know the future. He wandered in from time to time to wind up Bridget with his wit which was really sarcasm. She hated him and smacked his head with me. As fleeting and gentle as it was, I had his thoughts in me.

I am almost embarrassed by his story of wanton debauchery. I will tell it nonetheless as a warning.

Daphne was one of the people who wandered into his canvas dominion like a fly being caught in a spider's web.

'Sit down.' She obeyed. He then took his payment which made her eyes water but she wanted to know if she would meet a man who would be suitable for her after a lot of others who had just wanted her for her good looks and shapely body. She was at her wit's end. Men had courted her, used her and discarded her as if she was a commodity that would be put in a waste bin after they had pleasured their egos and more.

'Place your left hand in mine.'

She did.

He had read her as soon as she walked in. No engagement or wedding rings. Her look of distress and her timidity told him she was there to review her dreadful life with ex-lovers and she wanted hope about new ones, or with any luck, just one.

He moved his finger along the lines on her palm and talked about her life-line, heart line and interpreted her wrinkles with apparent knowledge and wisdom. He was well practiced in his act and she was hooked by the generalisations that seemed to resound with her.

'That is the past. Now the right hand for your future.'

Obeying without question, she swapped her hands. Again, he waffled on about things that might happen while his finger touched her hand more and more intimately.

She was on his baited hook.

'You know, I can only read so much from the hand. There is a better way.'

'What is that?' She asked, almost implored.

'I can tell the definite future from reading the nipple. You would not wish to do that, I am sure. Thanks for visiting. Bye.'

'No. I will do that if it tells the real future.'

She undid her blouse and pulled down her bra to expose her breasts. He went ahead with the reading, touching with his finger, then feeling a whole breast with his hand.

He told her so many lies that gave her hope about how love would find her in the shape of a rich handsome man who would love her for ever.

Intrigued, she wanted to know his name.

'I cannot tell you, but…'

He was interrupted by Bridget who burst into the tent.

'…it would be necessary to take your pants off and then later letting him screw you.' She shouted.

As Daphne restored her breasts to her bra and buttoned her blouse, Bridget walked over to the perverted man and prepared herself to slap him, but on second thoughts, punched him in the face. She broke his nose and blood poured down onto his shirt. He was crying.

'Don't worry, you nasty man, I know a faith healer who will fix that for you.' Bridget was angry, furious.

She waited for Daphne to regain her composure and then left the tent with her. 'He should have known that tents are not sound proof.' They both laughed together but poor Daphne was heartbroken at being let down by yet another man. Together they walked back to the small room that Bridget used as her refuge and spy hole to see what was going on.

She explained to her new friend what had happened and who had tried to make money from selling the impossible to know.

'This is the last one of these I will ever do. That is my future sorted.

Bridget handed me to Daphne to read. 'This probably won't help you to find a nice bloke but it will amuse you during the wait.'

As she left the room, one of the paramedics came back to collect something that he had left behind earlier. He was not rich but he was single, good looking and took a shine to Daphne. They chatted and in the following days, they courted, fell in love and wandered off into the sunset.

Actually, dear reader, I made that last bit up. I thought we needed a happy ending for this tale.

11
DIRTY BOOKS

I was one of the few publications that Malcomb had read that did not have pictures of naked women in them.

He had the sexual drive of a young man but lacked the looks and charm that would bring satisfaction with a real woman. He had partners but nobody who would bring herself to love him. Lovemaking was rapid and not a good experience for the women he bought who he called girlfriends but they called him a customer.

Now, after a number of difficult years, he had grown from being a buyer of sexual images to being a producer of them. It started when he persuaded an escort girl to pose as he was filmed in the act by a friend who was paid by using the same girl afterwards. The film was sold to his friends for favours and drugs and it occurred to him that there was a living to be made from selling rather than buying.

As you can see, I am free of porno-very-graphic images of couples having sex in a variety of ways that would have made the acrobats of Cirque du Soleil look like amateurs. As was my first printing.

He did not read much of me. I was beyond his imagination and ability to understand words rather than pictures. I was glad because I did not like the idea of being held by hands that had touched his body and the bodies of the numerous ladies of the night he had used, and porn stars he had groped in his business of making films of Viagra stoked penises being pushed into every available orifice of women who justified their profession as acting rather than being exploited. He put me in a corner of his room, the so-called studio, where his 'actors' would rest, have some drugs and get ready for the next part of the daily marathon.

Yes, Malcomb was a movie producer who sold his 2-dimensional thrills to people who were unable to get 3-dimensional people to lead a regular life with.

Much to my annoyance, I became part of his work quite unwittingly. One of the bed legs on his main prop had been damaged by the continual bumping, bouncing, bounding, springing and crashing of two or more bodies creating love free, love making.

Martha held me tight to her naked body as she crouched in a corner looking away from everything and just hiding by looking at the walls. I seemed to comfort her as she sat trying to blank out the noises of fake love in the background. She needed a different life away from the constant stabbing by a variety of pumped up penises that hurt her sense of self-worth as much as daggers. I was something she could hold on to without fear of forced sex or pain. So alone, I was the only company she had in the shadows from the big lights used to illuminate the sordid activities that happened in the studio.

The story of Martha was a sad one. She had been hooked on heroin since the age of twelve. She used it to escape from the abuse of her father and his friends who paid for the use of a young girl. She had exchanged that exploitation for her life as a porn star who was abused by men but some of the money made was given to her to support her drug habit. Her life was miserable

Malcomb saw she was distressed and walked over to her. He saw she was holding me and ripped me from her trembling hands

'Just what I needed.' He muttered as he walked away with no concern for Martha whatsoever. To him, she was just a component as if she were a sack of flour in a biscuit factory.

Lifting the corner of the bed, he put me under the leg to level the thing up. It was undignified for me to be used by the porn industry when all I did was absorb the stories of all the parties involved as they humped each other, took cocaine and drank extraordinary amounts of wine, whisky and whatever else that would hit me after being spilt or spat out.

I was published to entertain and inform, not as a film extra. I can see some of my other readers being excited by what they have read here but I know your reaction and it is not a strange one, just shock at what I was involved with.

My issue is that as a book, I am in the same broad category as other books. Yet every book is different in the same way that Malcomb's films were very different to Disney children's films.

What is not seen in a porn film is the suffering that the actors go through. Some of the men and women involved had read me in the 'green' room. The corner where they would prepare. Men would dose up on Viagra and the women would drink to make them numb and beyond feeling anything apart from doing the pantomime of having an erotic and exciting time even though they were in a cramped studio with mike booms and cameras filming every available part of their bodies.

The set up was as unromantic as watching meat being prepared in an abattoir before being cooked and served in a high-class restaurant. It was all about fake from beginning to end and the only thing that was real was the money Malcomb made from selling the lowest points of people's lives dressed up like Christmas turkeys. Once the glitter and shiny foil was removed, all that remained were porn 'stars' who had no other way to make a living.

With nobody to read me and for me to read their lives, I was alone in that place as if in a coffin made from my book cover that kept me trapped as a piece of the filthy furniture in that location where fantasies for watchers were made.

Within this tale there is no resolution. The porn industry will never end. The diverse needs of people who take part and who buy, will never be satisfied. The greed of the producers will ensure that the business will continue into the future and become more horrific.

I was glad when a new bed was bought and I was removed from the premises and given a home on the bookshelf of one of the actresses who had become too old to participate and earned a small living by scrubbing, dusting and washing the place after the films were shot. She found me with the debris from the old bed, took me away and I was able to comfort her in the only way I could; as a book for her to read.

Out of a sense of respect, her story is not told here.

12
IN THE NICK

I did not mind being in prison.

When I was not being read by Nick, there were lots of other people sharing our mutual reading moments. I became quite an expert in criminal activities from the knowledge I picked up from all sorts of men. I knew how to pick locks, how to break into houses, steal cars, and other robbery techniques. I was not happy when I read drug dealers and I was disgusted when touched by child abusers. I wished that my abilities, at those times, did not exist.

Nick was, and is, innocent of the crime he was jailed for. Lots of prisoners say that and there are some who are. I know he was because I could see inside his mind. I read his anger at being falsely imprisoned but I was also aware of his desperation at being separated from his children. His emotions were on full display. He missed Barbara, his wife and two young sons. He spent long days picking at his fingers and praying for the miracle that would bring the truth out so that he would be released from the stained concrete walls that held him in his physical and emotional trap.

His friend Peter never visited him. Nick did not know why until his wife told him that his best mate now lived in Spain. That did not cause any problems apart from envy that the two men who had been involved in a fight with Jo Scarlett, a drug dealer, were not treated the same after the assault. It was Peter who had bludgeoned the man in an alley. It was him who had caused the man to lose his ability to see and hear. My poor reader took the blame for that and Peter had not been caught. He had run away while Nick tried to give first aid to the victim of Peter's wrath. Nick was sentenced to ten years in jail. Ten years during which, he knew, his children would grow into their teenage years without a father. They would write letters from time to time that would be delivered with an ever-increasing time delay between each one. Barbara's visits became less frequent as time passed. That saddened Nick who saw his marriage falling apart.

When Barbara went on holiday, she took me with her to pass time on the flight. I was taken aback by the coincidence that she had bought me at the airport and then, unknowingly, delivered the other half of Nick's story to me.

I was not surprised to learn that she was going to Spain while the children stayed with her mother. It was after she had landed and she had gone through passport control that it was confirmed that she was being met by Peter. It seemed a nice thing for him to do for a friend. If I had a tongue, it would be in my cheek as I say that.

Barbara was driven to his villa and having dropped her bag in the bedroom, slipped on her bikini bottoms, made her way to the pool and dived in. Peter was lounging by the side with a big glass of gin and tonic resting next to one for her. He admired her body as she flipped and span to show off her breasts to tease him. She climbed out of the pool, slipped her bikini bottom off and sat next to him.

'Have you got your accounts?' He demanded as she picked up her drink.

'Why customs never check memory sticks is beyond me.' She laughed.

Later on, he opened his laptop and put the stick in. He read the accounts for her cosmetic company.

'Very good.' He murmured. 'I see the foundation powder is selling well. And the crystal sparkles. Well done.'

She was pleased and went for a shower and to dress for dinner. Peter, being what he is, went through her bag. He picked me up, opened my pages and flicked through. It was then that I read him.

If I was able to be shocked then I would have been. His life read like a horror and gangster film blended together to make a bloody cocktail. He had murdered, maimed, tortured and abused people all his life. He sold drugs through his cronies in Britain and they reported to Barbara.

With my knowledge of prison inhabitants, I was horrified that some of them were incarcerated and this man was free, living a life of luxury paid for by the blood and misery of his victims.

Her make up items were just euphemisms for the drugs. Face powders were cocaine, crystal sparkles were crystal meth. The list was big and long and the profits made from each item of their merchandise was carefully accounted for in their coded accounts that would be seen as nothing apart from a small enterprise with lots of the zeros in the numbers missing to make them look small.

When Nick was dating Barbara, the pair met Pete in a night club. There was immediate attraction but Pete was not into long term relationships and he found it better to reserve a woman by having her attached to a buddy who had no idea of what was going on behind his back. Sometimes the girls would succumb to the drugs and lush lifestyle that was offered when her regular partner was away on an errand set by Pete. Usually when they declared love, he would drop them. To Pete, that spelled danger. Barbara was an exception. She had a talent and she was able to help him to expand his business by her creative thinking. It was her who had warned him about Jo Scarlett expanding into Pete's territory. Pete asked his friend to accompany him on a night out and, unknown to Nick, they had wandered into the other drug dealer's patch. Pete needed a fall-guy, a scapegoat.

Everything went to plan, and relying on his friend not grassing him up, Nick was removed from the scene to allow Barbara more time to build the empire.

She was enjoying her holiday. She loved sunshine, Spanish

wine, seafood and the luxury of being flattered and made happy by a man she had known for many years. Her dream had been realised when she had met the man of her dreams while pretending that she had met that in Nick. Although he was sweet and kind and a good father to the two children, one of whom was actually Pete's, he lacked ambition and above all, lacked money to make her happy.

Pete was the man she wanted, the lover she would dream of when she made love with Nick. Even though her man had escaped justice and had run to Spain, his income was still gigantic from the business links, as he called them, operated without his physical presence. All his input was from his mind and his ability to use people to scare others into operating his plans.

She knew how to use her looks and her body to gather new recruits for the company. She would trap them with drugs and sex and once they had committed enough crime, then she would use blackmail. She was kept safe by a huge man, carefully selected by Pete as her gay minder. Even he would have felt jealous if his lady had been accompanied by a more sexually interested protector. While Nick was in prison, Pete's scheming would work like clockwork. He had no issues, strangely enough, with her sleeping with targets because they would end up hating this femme fatale after the event.

When the plain clothes police arrived, Pete and Barbara were both sunbathing naked next to the pool. They were arrested and told to dress before being taken to a small airport from where they were flown back to England in a private jet.

'Who are you?' Pete asked many times before and during the flight. He was very suspicious about the big policemen. They refused to answer until the plane landed.

'I am not a policeman, mate. My name is Mike Cooper which will mean nothing to you until I tell you that you nearly killed my brother, Jo Cooper.' Pete was still puzzled. 'He used to be known as Jo Scarlett. While you have been in Spain enjoying the high life paid for by people who got high on the stuff you sold them, my brother died as a result of what you did to him.'

Mike had been working with a policeman in the drugs squad and had made a very questionable deal that he would track down Pete and his accomplice and make them magically available for arrest in England without having to go to the bother of having them extradited. The choice for the policeman was to have them alive or to discover that two people had accidentally drowned in a swimming pool in Spain. This was against the law but it was in keeping with the laws of justice held in the policeman's mind. The lawyers could argue about Pete being abducted but the warrants for his arrest existed and it would be argued that there was no seizure, Pete had returned of his own accord to continue with his drug dealing and the violence that entailed, they would be told.

He was tried and found guilty of many crimes and was sentenced to twenty years in jail. His accomplice, Barbara, tried to bargain for her freedom but the names she gave were known to the police and were of no value. She was jailed for ten years.

The timing was good allowing a space of a month or two. Pete now occupied the cell that Nick had been in. His cell mate was an undisclosed friend of Nick's and passed me over for Pete to read. I had been a gift from Nick to his jail friend, Paul, who had heard the stories Nick told about his innocence and about the real villain.

It happened that Paul was also a friend of the Cooper family and had passed on what he had been told by Nick. Not believing him at first, he was still interested enough to have members of the old gang do some checking. Strangely enough, they also 'found' some 'witnesses' who proved Nick was innocent and that Pete was guilty. Through their own networks they had tracked Pete down to his villa in Spain.

After Nick had been released, he was able to be back with his children in a happy home. They write to their mother now and again in her new home, a prison where life is not luxurious. She is disliked by the other inmates whose men had been honey trapped by her wily ways and they took subtle but hurtful revenge on this woman who had been the cause of their misery.

Pete knew that prison can be a brutal and hostile place. He had made many enemies along his path of extortion, brutality, violence, murder and deaths from drugs.
Revenge is not always sweet; it can be bitter and hurts a lot when applied to a monstrosity.

13
INDIAN TAKEAWAY

Sitting on a plane in first class on my way to India suited me well.

Not that the luxury of being in the front of the plane made any difference to me. Yet it was preferable to being taken on holiday flights where, once there, my cover would be smeared with sun tan lotion and my pages made transparent. I could detect that when my reader did it.

I need to explain something. As I have said before, I am unable to read, see, hear, smell or taste. I have to pick up the thoughts of what my reader is sensing. So, if one reader loves haggis and another hates it, my reactions to the stuffed stomach rely on the person who has eaten it. It is the same as TV cookery programmes. People sit to watch food being prepared but they are unable to smell, taste or touch it but are overwhelmed by the skill of the chef. The audience has to be directed and guided by the tasters. For all the viewer knows, they could be praising a plate of dog excrement. I hope that this explains that my input is from the minds of my readers and my output is returning my collective experiences back to them and you in the words you are having read to you by your mind.

So, the next two weeks would be spent enjoying curries of all different types, depending on Dina Anand picking me up so that I could read him. In turn, I was being read by him, the businessman who had bought me to help him to escape from the hours that the flight took. It was different for me having no sense of time, although I spent a lot of it in the seat pocket in front of him. He had experienced a varied life having grown up in a home that was caring. He had been well educated and had worked hard and honourably to achieve his success. He was on his trip to find a partner for the import of clothing items that were made by workers who were treated with respect and given dignity in their employment. His potential business associate was Manish Gupta who had been recommended by a colleague who had been at school with him.

Dina checked into his hotel after clearing the airport. He was still clearing his head having flown over the slums as the plane landed. It seemed to just skim over the top of the fragile looking buildings that were threaded together to house an absolute mass of people.

He found the restaurant on the ground floor and sat to eat a meal that was so different from the food he ate at home. The flavours jumped at him from spices designed to enhance tastes rather than to heat the mouth. A cook twirled chapatis and threw them onto a heated dome to cook as if he was a gold medal winner in a new sport of precision. It was entertainment for the mind, mouth and his curiosity. Although he ate Indian food at home, here it was different. The ingredients more vegetable based than meat. The method of cooking was traditional to the home country and was not adjusted to western cooks and customers.

After his dinner Dina unpacked his case and went to bed. He sweated even in the air-conditioned room and found sleep difficult to find. Although I have no senses of my own, I enjoyed the meal very much by reading the reactions Dina had to the range of dishes he ate and how he recalled them as he searched for sleep.

The next morning, we went to a grand office at the other polar extreme to the slums. Everything was lavishly furnished and the employees smartly dressed to reflect their salaries in this exporting empire.

Within moments a beautiful woman (according to the thoughts I received) collected him and led him to the elevators that took him to the top of the building. He was then led into the office of

Manish and asked to sit in a big, soft leather chair. I sensed a power play was about to start. Manish was gently perfumed to be impressive rather than overpowering. His suit was expensive and made from fine material and tailored to perfection. The scene was set and the games started.

'This is a fine chair. The leather is so soft. Cow leather, I guess.'

Dina knew exactly what he had said and wanted to establish that he knew the man he was talking to acted against the culture he lived in.

'No. The cow is sacred in India as I am sure you know.'

They discussed the deal and Dina insisted that the workers in the factories were well looked after and treated kindly.

'They are. Of course. It is within the very fabric of my company that we are humane and caring for our staff, including the workers in our manufacturing plants.'

Dina had prepared a long list of questions that needed to be answered before any contracts were signed. As he opened his brief case, I fell out onto the table.

Manish picked me up and flicked the pages. 'I did not realise that a man of your stature would have such nonsense in his possession.'

He talked as if I had been a children's comic.

I took my opportunity to read him in just the few moments he held me.

It was as if the two extremes of the city were exposed but in a different dimension. At one end there was Dina, the honest and humanitarian businessman and at the other end, the dishonest abusing thief of the little dignity that poor people had. I also knew that on his rise to the top, he had arranged for people to be murdered. He had raped women and young girls and had shared them with his henchmen. He had families thrown out onto the streets which were only a little worse than the houses they lived in. He was not a nice man. He was a vile gangster, a villain and a crook of the highest order.

There I was, in the company of two opposites. I needed to help my friend before mistakes were made but I did not know how. Yet it is strange how things work.

After Dina had handed over his questionnaire to Manish, who would in turn hand it to his assistant to fill in, Dina arranged a visit to one of the factories for the following day. He would be collected from his hotel and driven to the site.

As he left the building there were beggars doing their best to collect small amounts of money to buy food for their families. Dina knew very well that there were syndicates of beggars run by bosses who took the proceedings and gave a small amount back. It was a racket where if the beggars tried to keep the money they had obtained, they would be punished by beatings or even killed.

One of them was a pretty woman in her twenties, he guessed. He gave her nothing and walked back through the crowded streets that smelled of human detritus.

As he was about to enter his hotel, she was there again. Her hands were waving, not for coins, but to attract his attention. Dina stopped and she spoke to him. 'He raped my mother and me many years ago.'

'Who did?'

'The man you have just seen, Gupta.'

Not sure how to react, he paused. These were serious allegations perhaps made by somebody who wanted to punish Gupta for unknown reasons.

Dina was a good judge of people and, intrigued, he invited her into the lobby; only for her to be refused admission by the doorman.

'But she is my guest.' Dina said.

'She is not allowed in here.' The big man replied while being worried that he was offending an important guest by suggesting that he wanted to bring a cheap woman of the night into the hotel.

Dina wondered if he was now in the company of a known prostitute who had been banned from his fine hotel.

'Why?' He asked.

'She is a poor woman not suited for this place. Her clothes are bad, her shoes are cheap.' Was the stern reply that covered his discomfort at the refusal.

Dina grabbed the woman's hand and without saying a thing, walked back into the main shopping area and stopped at a busy boutique. He walked in pulling her with him and told the assistant to dress Suhani in the finest clothing they had. 'After she has showered. I am sure you can arrange that.' He whispered to the shop's manager who had mysteriously appeared and pulled a face that incorrectly said that he knew what was going on. Dina growled at him and told him to learn some manners.

An hour and a half later, they returned to the hotel where Dina's new companion was welcomed.

'Now we can drink some tea.' He said.

As they sat in the restaurant, he asked her to explain to him what she had meant about Gupta raping her and her mother. He was patient and was happy to wait such a long time to hear her answers. It would be useful information about the character of the man who wanted to do business with him.

His Hindi was good but not perfect. She spoke some English which she had picked up along the way. She had wanted to progress in life and it was necessary to have an international language in her portfolio.

She explained that her mother and father both had worked in one of the factories that were owned by Gupta in his earlier days when he was building his kingdom of sweat shops. As a small child, she had to accompany her mother to work and was made to do repetitive tasks to earn permission to be there; she was given no money.

One day, Gupta visited, saw his mother and nodded to one of

his flunkies and walked straight on.

Later that day, at the end of her work shift late at night, her mother was dragged away. Suhani followed and was grabbed as well. They were taken to the office where they were raped. Suhani first by Gupta and then her mother while the girl was raped by the flunky.

They were then thrown out and threatened so they would keep their mouths shut. Shortly afterwards her mother and father were found dead on one of the many garbage dumps that existed in the city.

Suhani was raised by an aunt who taught her what she was able, including a smattering of English. Her aunt worked in a shop that served tourists and it was necessary to be able to speak bits of foreign languages.

She was in tears as she told Dina her story. He asked why she had waited so long to tell anybody and she replied that she had told many people in authority but had been advised to keep quiet because the defence of the very rich was a strong financial motivation for certain people.

She saw Dina as a kind man purely from her instincts of self-protection and she was prepared to take the risk she had. He was known in India for his charitable works and his picture often appeared in newspapers and magazines which were readily available blowing on winds in the roads and alleys.

Dina was a happily married gentleman with no base thoughts about the girl and promised that he would take care of her as if she was a newly discovered niece. He booked her a room where she would have the privacy and safety that she deserved.

They had breakfast together before his factory visit and she told him that the one he was going to see was dressed and prepared for buyers. It would appear to be a good place to work and the workers would have been bribed to appear to be happy and efficient. To discover the truth, he would need to go elsewhere and she suggested the workshop where her mother and father had worked.

As he left, he opened his case and gave me to her so that she could practice reading English. She smiled, put her hands together and thanked him. Then on a pure whim, she kissed his cheek and returned to her room.

When he returned, he was disappointed at what he had seen. It was all too perfect and his request to visit other factories was declined politely with a series of weak excuses. The completed questionnaire was handed to him in an envelope together with a draft contract. He was a catch for manufacturers as he owned clothing outlets that dressed people from the hat down to the shoe with everything in between. His products catered for men and women from shirts, trousers, underwear and belts.

As he ripped up the contract, Suhani appeared and looked excited. 'Today I met my uncle who is the manager of a factory that makes clothing. We had lost contact but he walked in here for a meeting with his boss. I looked so pretty in the clothes you bought for me that he invited me to sit in with them. I was worried at first because of what had happened with the other factory owner that I told you about. We all sat together and Ajay Desai seemed to be an honest man who respected others. He was meeting my uncle because he had performed well at managing the factory, setting up social activities for the families of the people who worked there and he wanted to buy him lunch and to talk about my uncle advising the other factory managers on how staff worked better when they were treated well. Unlike the monster, Manish Gupta, who was being investigated on numerous charges of wrongdoing including trying to defraud companies who are interested in buying goods from him. I was told that in confidence, by the way.'

She smiled at Dina. 'He liked your book and I let him read a few pages. I was carrying it for comfort. I hope you don't mind,

Uncle Dina.' Her smile lit the hotel like a bright summer sun.

To cut an already long story short, I read Suhani and she was as genuine as was her real uncle, and Ajay Desai. It was an easy step for Dina to meet up with the honest and compassionate factory owner and his deal was set.

Back in England a few months later, Dina was going through a few bits and pieces and when he picked me up to put away safely, I learned that Suhani was engaged to Ajay Desai's son. I also read that Manish Gupta had fallen to his death in a tragic accident that was not explained fully.

I need somebody who knows more to read me in India to explain how a man's scrotum had been trapped in a leather dressing machine. Had it been Suhani who had arranged for it to happen, then I would have known.

It was obvious that the vile man had a forest of enemies and a tree had fallen on him, at last. I was unable to read Gupta in the moments before his death. He just closed down on me, so the mystery remains.

After his demise, his factories were acquired by Ajay and were run ethically and humanely as were other factories bought by other manufacturers. Mumbai had become a little cleaner from the day Gupta left. I hope that in his reincarnation, he comes back as he deserves.

14
OUT OF PRINT

I will tell you more about why the first book was taken out of print at my request. Actually, I had to do certain things that were difficult to perform.

I had been shocked at what I saw inside people. I was unable to make physical efforts to make changes so I needed to find a way to influence transformation. What people do and what they say are very different at times. Most people never express what they really feel. I was able to penetrate the barriers in the mind and see what was hiding there.

With that first publication, the reader had no realisation that they were being read but there was something going on that affected them. I needed to remove myself because it was unfair that I was reading people without their knowledge. In this book, I came clean from the start and the choice to read and be read could be made.

I lost contact with my previous readers but I had all the knowledge about them in me. I know now that taking the previous book out of print was an attempt to destroy the information that had been given away. It could not happen, however. It was stored in me.

In the end, I withdrew my printed words and the publishers had nothing to sell. Computer glitches and human errors were blamed but the manuscript disappeared as did all the files and records. I achieved my aim of being out of circulation.

What was left was a demand for a new publication but before that happened it was necessary for me to be able to devise methods to have a two-way conversation with my readership. I could read them and they could read my words but I needed them, you, to be able to pick up meanings from what was seen unconsciously with their emotions as well as consciously with processing the stories that came from before.

Hence the stories gleaned from those who read the first book have been chosen to point ways through the shared issues that people have in common.

Why should I, you ask? Simply so that I get to know even more about even more people. The purpose has no purpose. It is just something that I do.

Perhaps you think that I am a voyeur in electronic or paper form. No. A voyeur looks at privacy for their own personal gratification and sense of uncovering what is normally concealed. I get nothing from seeing naked people. I am a book and cannot get excited even seeing another book without its cover. Sorry for the joke.

I am more like a reporter who sees much but tells a little for information rather than for exposure. The stories here are told to show what can go right and wrong in the lives of people. They are aimed at helping my readers, perhaps entertaining them, but I cannot decide how you, dear reader, will respond. And I am also aware that some reporters sell secrets for profit. Not here. What would I do with money? I cannot use it.

In my first book, I read the misery and joy that lives in people. I felt that it was necessary to dispose of those emotions and feelings that I saw by removing myself from circulation. After I had, they still continued as thoughts and memories. The way forward for me was to return as a publication that would reach out to my readers of old, some of whose stories are told here, and to show the results of follies and the joys of taking opportunities to a new audience.

I feel as if I am writing myself, as if I am the taker of dictation that will turn into printed words. The difference between you and me is that you have to read he whole book to reach the end and to know what happens. For me, I read my readers in an instant. As I said before, I have no idea how or why. It just happens. There is no logical explanation I can give you. I exist outside of logic and it is as simple as that. I am one book but I am also the infinity of the copies of me that are picked up and read and of the people I read.

And as a note, I refused blank pages between the stories in order to show respect for the planet by saving the trees that would have been chopped down to make paper that had no purpose other to make this book look prettier. Ha! Not necessary.

I wonder at times whether or not I am a parasite. I read people without their permission and I use what I discover to tell other people what has happened in those lives. In that way I am no different to a mosquito, a leech or a tick if you close the definition of a parasite to a base level. You could go even further because, as I am doing now, I put things into the readers' minds like a mosquito spreads malaria and a tick can give its host Lyme disease.

Yet how would it be if a creature took blood and gave something back for the benefit of the giver? Blood donors give in return for satisfying a sense of welfare for others and a cup of tea with a biscuit. The Blood Donation service is not parasitic. It is a benevolent service that saves lives.

The human parasites are those who take without giving anything in return. They cause harm by using others to make their lives easier without returning anything to them.

So, if you think that I am a parasite in book form, let me apologise. You chose to read me and I did say in my first few words that I can read you. Our exchange of information is between us. Your doctor would never be thought of as a parasite when he or she knows a lot about you which is kept private. The stories I relate to you are hidden enough to make them explanatory of certain things without being specific, unless, uh hum, they are to expose parasites of society, human and other animal kind or the whole life of the planet in general.

May I suggest to you that what I would like to be seen as is a symbiotic thing. In that there is an advantageous exchange. As a bee takes pollen in return for fertilising a flower and the pilot fish that cleans a shark of parasites in return for protection, there is a mutually helpful relationship.

I hope that I am being symbiotic in as much as you are enjoying reading stories that might just shine a light on yourself or other people and in return, I get to know you as a new friend. Come what may, a parasite, a mosquito never makes a choice about who they will take from and a symbiotic entity like me can never choose who reads me and I cannot pick who I read.

I needed to explain all of that. Thank you for listening to my thoughts. I will continue now with more stories that might or might not touch you. We, that is you and me, will see.

Please accept that I am proud to be read by eyes of every colour, every gender, every age, every race. But like ships they cannot comment on the cargo they carry; I make no judgements according to anything apart from what is held in the mind as characteristics of love or hate; generosity or greed; peace or war.

I do not look for the vulnerable or needy. It just occurs and I tell people what they need to hear in general terms.

15
TWO SIDES TO EVERY STORY

One side of the story.

It was talent night at the local bar. There were dreams of becoming a star. Aspiring entertainers would perform to their best and win the admiration of the crowds.

The first one up was the comedian. Graham told his jokes with the precision of a surgeon. Each one timed to perfection, the punch lines delivered with skill. Every joke was new to the audience. They loved him. He was a star. His talents were enormous. Although some people were unable to find the funny side of his gags, he felt sorry for them lacking the intellect to get the jokes.

Next was Stuart. He started to sing. Pitch perfect, he added emotion where it was needed and the audience stood aghast at the way he sang ballads, new pop and old rock songs. They loved him. He took his bows and joined his new gathering of fans. He was appreciated and his natural flair was a gift. He was proud that he had never taken singing lessons; he was totally self-taught.

Then Stan took to the stage and danced to the rhythm of the music. He span, he leapt; he had the crowd in the palm of his hands as they stood open mouthed in admiration at the nimbleness and athleticism of this man at his best. He knew he should apply to the big talent shows where his art would be recognised. Maybe he would be given his own show that would attract millions of viewers.

Finally, Fred told his stories about how he had become a champion boxer. He related his tales of how he had started, how he had become motivated and what his killer punches were and how he used them to such great effect. He still knew how to box and from time to time he sparred with younger men he met to encourage them. They seemed to have a high regard for his proficiency at throwing a punch and also for being able to take them.

In the audience, Alan was pleased with the way it had gone as he continued talking to Joan, a beautiful young blond who he had charmed all through the evening. He was wearing his best mohair suit and the most expensive after shave that emphasised his good looks. He had seduced this beauty and was going to take her home to demonstrate his proficiency at love making. He knew she liked him very much.

While he carried on talking to his gorgeous conquest, the four entertainers gathered together, had a drink and talked about how the evening had gone. They were a mutual admiration society. Egos came to the fore and they all agreed that they were fantastic in their own spheres of showbiz.

It was time to leave. They said goodbye to each other as audience praised them one by one as they walked away to return to their homes.

All in all, five men left that place feeling good.

George, the manager of the pub, introduced the acts who had volunteered to take part. The crowd was made up from regulars and a number of new visitors. It was in aid of selling more food and drink in an otherwise difficult market where folk would buy their drinks from cut-price supermarkets and consume it at home in front of the television that offered such diverse amusement. George wanted to offer variety.

The other side of the story.

Graham hit the stage first as an act George hoped would warm the audience up. He was a little unsteady on his feet as he grabbed the microphone and told his first joke. It was racist and full of four-letter words as were the ones that followed. In his act no minority was left out. People of colour, Jews, Muslims, the disabled, lesbians, gay men and transgender folk featured in his act.

No profanities were ignored. They were repeated over and over and over. After the first few jokes were told with no laughter, there was just the sound of booing and shouts of, 'Get him off'. He was ejected from the stage by two hefty doormen who threw him onto the pavement outside.

Stuart took to the stage nervously after downing two more double whiskies which were 'on the house' and slurred through the first song. He was badly out of tune. The only relief for the audience was when he forgot the words and the recorded backing track played on and they sang along. Again, the doormen stood by but Stuart got off the stage, went to the bar, ordered more whisky before being refused and told to leave.

When the next singer got onto the stage, he did well despite the idiotic prancing of Stan who, not having a stage act that would be respected, swept his arms through the air, twirled, jumped and pirouetted to the music before falling over onto his face. He, like the other two drunks, was ousted from the bar. The good singer continued on and was met with loud applause.

Fred thought he was tough. He made threatening noises at anybody who came near him or his strong lager, the love of his life. He was not a welcome visitor and when he tried to throw a punch at George for telling him to behave himself, he was also evicted by the doormen after telling them that he could beat both of them in a fight. He could not. They grabbed his flailing fists and threw him, somewhat heavily onto the pavement where he vomited.

Meanwhile, while all that was going on, Alan was annoying Joan. His scruffy jeans and shirt were covered in dribbles. The shirt from saliva, the jeans from urine. Joan was indeed a pretty woman but had no interest in the insane behaviour and chatter of a drunk who thought he was ready to become the next James Bond. Reeking of alcohol rather than the after-shave he imagined, he stalked her. Wherever she moved he followed until, at last, her boyfriend arrived and sat next to her. Alan, ever hopeful and deluded that she liked him, carried on prattling away. He thought he was victorious when her boyfriend stood up and walked away. His victory was well won, he thought, until Joan's beau returned with the doormen who took Alan away and added him to the human refuse tip outside.

The escape to a different world is easy for a drunk. The harsh facts of life can be obliterated and the stumbling mind is forced into a fantasy world where the only person living there is the one who can see positives.

It is a happy world that needs to be lived in all the time rather than visited now and again. There, the inebriated and befuddled person is a happy, entertaining and philosophical deep thinker about life. The change is not necessarily noticed by others when the drunkard learns how to disguise the intake of booze, but it is felt. Very often the most sober seeming person is actually the most drunk.

When Graham eventually got home, his children were crying.
'What's the matter with them?' He shouted at his partner.
'You have come home.' Was her reply.
He took the bottle of vodka he had stolen from the pub out of his coat pocket and started swigging its contents. 'If the kids won't

shut up, then I'll either kill them or drown the noise out with this.' He pointed at the bottle as his partner cried yet again at the fate of the man who had once been pleasant and entertaining when he was sober in their earlier days. Now he was a hollow being who could only run away from life by drinking their money away so that the children would go hungry to finance his boozing. It was of no consequence to him.

Stuart made his way to a nearby bench, sat, slumped and fell asleep. He lived in many different places. Some were safer than others and he knew where he might be immune from being attacked, beaten and kicked. He knew all the songs he had tried to sing when he was in musical theatre years before but now, he could never remember the lyrics when he wanted to. He would sleep, dream of the old days when he had a wife and a nice home. Then he would wake up early, lonely and dry. He would do his best to adjust his life to suit the opening times of the shops he frequented who made the choice between serving a drunk for profit and taking the money he had stolen or begged, or encouraging him to seek help before he died.

Stan stumbled away to a shelter run by a church. He knew that one day the Almighty would bring about his salvation. Until then he would spend the time waiting by drinking. His past had been totally wiped out from drinking fake vodka that was fortified by the makers with anything they could find from anti-freeze to methylated spirits. Stan was once an eccentric until his need to be different became too much for him and he changed to the ultimate degree with the help of his liquid friend that made him forget whatever it was he had forgotten already.

Fred got home, or what he thought was home. A small scruffy terraced house where his wife would hide when she knew he would be getting back. Years before, he would greet her with a kiss, now the norm was a punch to the ribs where it would not show to the neighbours, although he forgot her screams could be heard. She hated her life but hated Fred more. Yet she had nowhere to run. She had tried before but he would find her, drag her home and punish her wrongdoings. He had been a moderate boxer in his earlier days but was beaten too many times by tougher men. He never had that problem with his wife.

Alan staggered away, not sure where to go. He could not figure out why somebody as handsome and charming as himself could be alone and single. Women were foolish not to recognise his talents and allure. He justified it to himself by assuming that women who did not fall for him must be lesbians who needed a good, sturdy and virile man in their lives. He was amazed by how many lesbians he met in the world these days.

When he was younger, he had girlfriends but as he got older, he had none. 'Must be something in the water that has changed them all. Thank God I only drink whisky. I don't want to become a dyke.' He laughed to himself as he fell to the ground in the middle of nowhere

Dear reader, I have no idea how those men found me or what became of them. Perhaps I read them by chance when they all managed to pick me up in random places. Or maybe they looked at one copy dropped in the gent's urinal. Who knows why or how they tried to read me or where they found me? The point is, I know or knew them although reading a drunk is difficult because they think in strange ways and it was like being drunk with them. Even their thoughts are slurred. The self-deception they had fooled me at times and I would get the feeling that they were misunderstood good men but when reality hit me, I just felt very sorry for the wasted lives they had found and how the effects influenced others just as badly.

It would be an ideal solution if I could tell you that they all got better, joined Alcoholics Anonymous and recovered their lives but the truth is that is unlikely. I have no idea what their fates were.

16
MOANER

In France, the name Mona means love.

For the inhabitants of her village tucked away in Aquitaine, it meant something different.

When she found the book in the boulangerie, I actually belonged to somebody else. Nobody noticed and the original reader had left me there by mistake while getting croissants for his family. On their way to the countryside after a long drive from England, they were hungry and in need of a snack. They would get to the gîte shortly but wanted food for now. They would do a full shop later. Not a great French speaker, Julian, a paramedic, was partly surprised that the names for breads and cakes were the same in both languages, although borrowed by the British. Pain au raisin, pain au chocolate. Then gateau, petit pain, tarte, meringue and so on. The amazing choice of baguettes astounded him. Rows and racks showed a huge variety of what the Brits know as bread.

Mona was in the queue behind him and thought it was her right to steal me as her reward for being kept waiting by a 'roast-beef', the derogatory equivalent of 'frog' for the French.

After she had bought her pain aux céréales, she slipped me into her bag. When I explain that I can understand all languages in the world, it sounds boastful. What I read are thoughts rather than words so I could read Mona as well as anybody else. She took me home and planted me on a sideboard and then put me back in her bag. She had no intention of reading a book, let alone one written in a foreign tongue. I was her trophy.

Like every small village in France, this one had a mayor. He was friendly and helpful. Easily approached, he went about his duties with efficiency and professionalism but every week Mona would go to the mairie with a new complaint. The cockerels were too loud in the mornings and dogs barked from time to time if they spotted a rat or a rabbit in the gardens where they lived. Perhaps it would be that the neighbour's leaves were falling in her garden in the autumn, or somebody had parked too close to her house. The list goes on for ever.

For other people her simple existence in the countryside would have been idyllic but for her nothing was good enough. She had been married but her husband had found somebody else who was happy with life. She was bitter at the betrayal as she perceived it. That bitterness flowed like vinegar into every part of her life. The plants, the lawn, the bread never responded but she needed reaction. Other people had to pay her back. There were two choices for her. She could become contented and jovial or, better for her, she could spread her discontent like she was broadcasting germs that would cause an epidemic. She was not aware of the antidote.

The villagers would vent their negative feelings onto her, feel better, walk away and laugh when they reported what had happened to others.

Once a young and radiant woman, she had developed a reserve around her that kept others away as well as a mediaeval fort. Any suitors she met were considered as potential rapists and violators of her perfect self. She would report men to the gendarmes or the maire as if they had committed a sin when all they had done was to compliment her in the hope she could be unfrozen from her ice-maiden state of body and mind. Eventually nobody cared and the whole village ignored her. Even the maire, a kind and caring man, had enough. He told her that as she lived in a rural place that had wild and farmed animals, she should accept that they lived in the ways they did. Cockerels would not be silenced; cows would moo as they were herded for milking. Woodpeckers would tap away at trees looking for their food and collar doves would make their monotonous cooing noise as they sat on the telegraph wires singing to their mates.

The day she fell over on her mile-long walk to the bakers, she sat on the pavement making loud groaning noises. The passing villagers walked around her. 'She is probably complaining about the quality of the stones that have been used.' They thought.

Julian was jogging to the bakers as a balance between fitness and the purchase of cakes and buns that had a lot of butter and sugar in them. He saw Mona on the ground and stopped. He was not aware of her reputation or the dislike there was for the woman that had been self-made.

In his meagre French, he tried to talk to her but she had no feelings for foreigners and despite her pain, she refused even an attempt to help her. In any event, he managed to get her to her feet, checked that there was no damage that would require a hospital visit and she limped away as he started to jog to his goal.

After he had bought his bread and cakes, he ran back in the direction of the gîte. He did not see Mona and thought she must have returned to her home wherever that was.

When he got back his wife opened his paper bags and poured coffee for her and Julian and orange juice for the children. Over breakfast, he told Julie about the strange woman he had found slumped on the ground. 'She wasn't old, about mid-thirties, but she wore the face of an old person.'

'C'est la vie.' Julie smiled. 'By the way, there is a dinner and some music at the village hall tonight. Shall we go? Children are welcome.'

At six o'clock that evening, the family walked to the salle des fêtes where they were greeted warmly. Holiday makers were bringers of money to the locality and added value to the wine making businesses that were the regular providers of local incomes.

The meal was good and was washed down with the local red wine. Julian was speaking to the mayor who had a good grasp of English. He asked if the woman he had found earlier was alright. 'Yes, she is fine. She fell over and hurt her ankle but she is OK. Of course, Mona, her name, came to see me to complain about the shoddy workmanship that caused her to trip. She likes to talk about trivial things like that.' He smiled and moved to speak with some of the other diners.

Julian returned to his seat and told Julie that the woman was alright. Her name is Mona, by the way. His daughter looked for the translation in her dictionary. 'Râleuse is the French word for moaner.' They all guffawed.

'That is what she is called behind her back and to her face.' The woman opposite them at the table said, giggling. My name is Joanna, I am a Brit married to a Frenchman. We live in the village and Mona is well known and not liked by anybody here.'

Julian and his family introduced themselves to Joanna and her husband. After what had been said about Mona, they had held their laughter until Julie started and it escaped from all of them.

'By the way, Julian, this book must be yours. It fell from the moaner's bag when she tripped and it has your name in the front. She dislikes all animals even though she acts like a thieving magpie when it comes to obtaining things.'

And so, I was returned to Julian. I had been a present from his wife for him to read on holiday and he was the sort of man who knew the value of a gift, not in monetary terms but in the thoughtfulness and kindness behind it. I was glad to share the remaining days of the holiday where the family enjoyed the clean air, the good food and the sunshine.

Their break went quickly, as they always seem to and I was sad for my family when I was packed for the drive back to England.

17
LOST FOR WORDS

'The impenetrable inflexible state of reality haunts all of us who cannot envision transformation.'

One Sunday afternoon, Martine was reading those over complex words over and over again as if she was stuck in a memory loop.

Too profound, too incomprehensible, too idiotic, too mind grabbing. Confused, she struggled to find reason. She decided to pass over the words and read on, but she was stuck. Over and over the words jumped at her and held her fixed, like the hypnotic stare of a king cobra. Dangerous and menacing, yet fascinating.

She had no reason to be scared by words, she had used them since she could speak. She thought with them, she understood their meaning. She was bright and intelligent. Yet she was unable to work out what those words that transfixed her mind were attempting to say to her. She put me down on her lap and decided to stop reading. Yet I was in her mind as the supplier of the words that haunted her.

She cursed me, threw me to the floor, stamped on me and then picked me up again and re-read those words. She tried turning the page but the same words hit her again as if the book, me, had been badly printed to repeat the page she was trapped on for ever.

She wasn't sure if she liked books or not. They were good to read but difficult to write. Her attempt at a novel failed after she was bogged down with the puzzle about how the princess who wed a dragon was able to consummate their marriage. It could have been transformed into a horror story but she gave up.

And her poetry was about how miserable her life was without

the person the poem was written for.

> Trickle tear, blind my eye that sobs away.
> Sweet tear that runs to my mouth
> And touches it no softer than he should.
> Mouth kiss brandy to forget
> What never shall be forgotten.
> I mean you.

She had sent it to her now ex-boyfriend to receive a short reply, 'Am I bovvered?'

Martine needed to escape from a boring job and a stagnant life. Reading was a pleasure for her because her mind was diverted by her images of landscapes, handsome men, adventures and excitement, but when she ended a book her life reverted to the way it was, and as far as she could fathom, would be.

Her loneliness was always worse on Sundays. The only lovers she had were the imaginary boyfriends she had sex with in the shower. Beforehand she would dress in her finest lingerie and slowly undress in front of her mirror watching her dream lover reacting to her curves and moving to caress her as she entered the warm stream of water with him washing her body with his hands.

Afterwards, the redness of her blue eyes from the shampoo and soap was maintained by her tears of isolation from an unfulfilled life.

On those days that brought the close of the weekend, she would always eat a take-away pizza washed down with a bottle of wine. Then any film apart from a romcom that ironically seemed to emphasise her lack of romance and comedy.

Returning to the words that ensnared her, she wrote them down in a column. She defined each word and wrote its meanings next to it. No help whatsoever.

On the Monday morning she took me to her office to pass time during her lunch hour. Jim, a colleague who she liked very much, sat next to her and asked what she was reading.

She showed him and he told her that he had read me recently. I knew him.

'Did you get stuck on any of the words? She asked in the hope that it was not her but a bad piece of writing that made no sense whatsoever.

'No, I didn't, but there was a sentence that intrigued me and I figured out what it meant. It was pretentious in the way it was penned but it became clear after I sorted the muddle out.'

'Which bit was that?' Martine demanded rather than asked.

'Give me the book, please.'

She handed me over to the man next to her. He flicked through my pages and immediately found where Martine had become captured. It was easy because my pages at that point were spread by her constant searching for a meaning.

'That bit.' She pointed at the sentence. It's that one.'

He said slowly. 'Basically, the words say if you want something to happen, then get off your arse and do it or otherwise nothing changes.'

The meaning of the snooty sentence hit her.

'Do you fancy dinner tonight?' She asked Jim.

'That was unexpected but very welcome. I wanted to ask you but I was not sure how you would respond.'

Martine smiled. 'Well you should have got off your backside and asked me before.' They chuckled.

She gave him her address and set a time. She cooked, opened a bottle of wine so it could breathe, showered and put on her smartest dress. Her makeup was perfect and she sat sipping her wine until the doorbell rang. Jim was there with a big bunch of flowers and two books.

'I know you like reading so I brought these for you.'

She did not have a literary evening in her mind and she poured him some wine, put the flowers into a vase and fussed around getting her starter onto the table.

They ate well, drank well and chatted away until it was late. He said he had to go but they arranged to meet on the following Friday at her place again.

They kissed and then kissed again for longer and he went away. Too polite to ask if he could stay the night, he left reluctantly but was hopeful for the next date. Besides, it was Monday and they both had work the following day.

Martine wondered if she should have asked him to stay but thought it would make her seem too easy. She was hopeful for their next date.

On the Friday evening, she cooked, opened a bottle of wine so it could breathe, showered and put on her sexy underwear. She hoped that she, or preferably he, would remove her fine silky underclothing slowly later.

'The impenetrable inflexible state of reality haunts all of us who cannot envision transformation.' She said to herself and laughed out loud. Her transformation had taken place.

18
SEEKING HIS DESTINY

Frank wanted his life to change substantially. He really needed it to improve.

He went to the online retailer and ordered me and two other books that he thought would help.

After my delivery on the Thursday after, he decided to read me, picked me up and had a look at my first few pages. He replaced me on his table and decided to look at me for diversion after reading the other two when they arrived. I was not worried. I had his thoughts already. A lonely man with few friends who were genuine buddies. He wanted more money so that he could buy clothes and other things he saw as luxuries. Even though he worked hard, he was always struggling. His friends always seemed to have much more than he did.

They were the same as him but to Frank, they were blessed by something that he lacked. Searching the Internet, he discovered that he was not being mindful enough or demanding his desires from the Universe. That was it. He had the answer. He needed to involve the power of the Universe in order to achieve and benefit from the abundance that others had but that he lacked. The solutions to achieving his needs were going to be held in the two books.

I was not the book he needed. I was an entertainment, a passing pleasure, something to read in order to relax its readers. I was not the golden key to happiness via extra cash.

On the Friday evening he opened the package containing the books he was excited about. Not sure which method to follow first, he tossed a coin, a good thing to involve money in his decision, he thought. He picked up the book that would manifest riches for him. All he had to do was sit quietly and see his future unfold with what he wanted. The Universe would provide for him. He had to see the outcome of his wishes rather than ask for money, the transient thing that had no place in this new world he was about to discover.

He saw the things he desired as if looking through a catalogue. He could choose anything, or should he avoid being greedy, he wondered.

He spoke his wishes out loud, in his head and even wrote them down. He had been instructed to ask once, visualise the outcome and then relax and wait. Were verbalising and writing going to work because they might be requesting his goals in two ways? He meditated and did everything to bring about a better life for himself.

To pass the time before his wished-for things came to him, he looked at the other book which told him to sit, relax and think about the moment. The past had gone and the future would happen. Ignore both and live just in the moment.

He was confused. The conversation with the Universe involved thinking about the future but he was told not to by the other book.

His other problem was that the future was what he wanted to think about and how he would spend his money that was being given to him by the powers of the Universe. Yet, if he did that then he would not achieve peace of mind and would be in a state of disturbance which might interfere with his plans.

I could understand his problem by reading what he had put into his head. Unable to assist directly, I had to let him work it out for himself. What had happened was that he wanted something to occur that was other worldly as his prayers had been in the past with similar results. Pray and wait for the miracle. It never has worked that way. Asking assumes that there is a patron of your life who is a wishing well. Why not assume a genie exists and you need to know the special touch or words to release it so that your requests will be fulfilled? People would be happy to sell you those magical secrets.

If these things are positive forces then they would recognise the need and supply what is needed without being asked. If that happened then wars would end and never be started. Hunger that kills millions in the world would be resolved so all could feed, rich or poor.

Over centuries, people have prayed, wished, hoped and begged the Universe, the gods and the spirits to stop the killing and hurt but it still goes on.

There is no proof that wishful thinking achieves anything. The thread that holds these things together is the requirement of individuals to invoke something outside themselves to do what those people are unable to do and in asking and waiting, the main method is missed.

It is certainly necessary to look to the future to perceive what is needed but rather than manifesting it in a mystic way, it rests with the planning for how to get it yourself. If somebody wants more money, they have to either earn more or spend less. If somebody wants good health then they should exercise, stop smoking, lose weight. If they want to find somebody to love they need to go to places where they will find like-minded people.

Schemes and plans for achieving goals make money for the inventors, practitioners and teachers of the enchanted route to success, wealth and happiness

No people who have made their affairs profitable have sat in their offices and imagined the money flowing in. Those people sat in their chairs and thought about what is needed by others, how to make life better for others, how machines, devices and gadgets could be improved to make them more attractive.

The secret is there for all to see. Decide what you want and then work towards getting it. Invent, improve or make available what is on offer to those who want things.

Frank was disappointed by his lack of success. Nothing suddenly came to him that made him better off. Women did not come his door delivering postal parcels and then fell in love with him. The shop assistant he liked in his nearby convenience store never asked him for a date.

Not one to give up, one evening he sat in his garden and immersed himself in his thoughts that were between empty and negative.

He felt pain on his leg, then his arm and on his face. Slapping at the mosquitoes that were long gone, he went inside.

He had a thought. He could either manifest the pests away from his life or, the light went on in his head, he could invent, develop or improve ways to trap or destroy mosquitoes.

Then he realised the difference between wanting and doing.

19
THE EMPEROR'S WINE

A rosé by any other name would taste the same.

I love the story I read in Stephanie. She had noticed that wine connoisseurs seemed to have upper class accents as if tasting wine changed the structure of the vocal cords. It amused her, a good middle class and middle-aged woman who had travelled extensively for her work. She had eaten the speciality foods of many countries and had drunk wine from the allegedly best to locally made wines that had love and affection in every sip.

To her delight she observed the folk who would look at the label first to appraise its cost and then they would go through the pantomime that followed.

Once in the glass, look at it. See the colours.

Smell it in the glass while it is on a flat surface.

Lift it, swirl it and then sniff again.

And, at last, take a sip.

Her father had grown up in the West of England and drank the product made from the local crops there, apples. She never saw him perform the routine with cider. He might sniff it briefly before pouring the golden, sometimes cloudy, liquid into his mouth and feel it trickle down into his stomach.

In London, the competition between wannabe alpha males was intense. It was not just about their money; it was also about cultural values because they came from breeding and one's pedigree was as valuable as if they had been at a human Crufts.

They would go through the performance as dramatic and intense as an opera.

Stephanie would attend a tasting at her friend's apartment

when she wanted to cheer herself up by inwardly laughing at the players in the game.

'I bought this in the Medoc from a dealer who had stored it in his cellar for fifteen years. Cost a bomb, but it is wonderful. Have a taste.' Ludlow stated to the small collection of ultra-rich guests.

So, they looked, sniffed, swirled, sniffed, and sipped.

'I'm getting oak from the barrels. A little bit of tannin.'

'Well, I'm getting red fruits and roses.'

'Yes, you are right. And I'm getting tobacco.'

Cecil, always a believer that there was, is and never should be any respect for women, looked at Stephanie. 'How about you?' He sniffed, not the wine, but with not very well concealed contempt.

She tasted without all the rigmarole after taking a sniff, more to answer Cecil's tone than for the wine and replied. 'I get farmyard.' They all sniffed and tasted and had to agree. 'And I am getting antique shop.' They again sniffed, tasted and nodded their agreement. 'And now I am getting the smell of leather in a brand-new Mercedes.'

She was making it up and chuckling at the puppet show where they dipped their heads to smell and then tipped them back to drink like the nodding drinking duck toy.

'Ooh. Wait a moment. Now I am getting spices and herbs that describe the warm countryside where the wine was made.' More nodding, sniffing and drinking. Stephanie struggled to keep a straight face.

'Ludlow. Have you any other wines for us?'

He went to his wine cellar where he kept his collection at the recommended temperatures and returned with a bottle.

'I know it is only a South African wine, but your opinion would be welcomed.'

Stephanie was puzzled that he had apologised.

If their displeasure had been audible the noise would have been deafening.

The second act in the circus was about to begin. The tasters dismissed the quality of wine by its label rather by its smell or taste. They knew that the price of the best South African wines would not match the French ones.

'Sorry Ludlow, but I think this is not up to scratch, old boy. Where can we spit it out?' Wigbert asked.

A spit bucket was produced and used by all apart from Stephanie who swallowed the excellent shiraz she had in her glass.

'Sorry about that chaps.' Ludlow apologised again as if he had served arsenic. 'I will get another bottle.'

He returned with a Californian wine. The same thing happened. Sipped and spat out. Stephanie liked hers though.

Ludlow was stuck. He wanted to present a global tour of wines but his guests, bar one, were fixed on the most expensive looking wines that he could offer.

Another French wine, this time a burgundy was enjoyed by everybody apart from Stephanie who used the spit bucket. It was too old and tasted awful.

Ludlow told them his show was over and they should now taste the wines the guests had brought with them.

Figgy was first with a Chablis that was excellent but which should have been drunk before the reds.

Ormorod was braver. He had an Australian red that was very drinkable but lacked something that none of them could define apart from Stephanie who, in her head thought, a high price. Her mention of a hint of eucalyptus got them all sniffing, swirling and sipping again. They started to like it better.

Kenneth stuck out, not just because he had a name without a price tag on it, but for the simple reason that he brought a Rioja. The men remembered the cheap Spanish wine they used at parties in their youth to get drunk quickly.

'Got the oak in this one, by Jove. Very nice.' Ludlow wanted to mention the oak because his first bottle had been oaky and well received.

Nobody spat that one and they took their time to discuss and evaluate the Spanish contribution.

Then, last but not least, Stephanie produced her bottle. It was French but the label did not shout 'expensive'. It was poured, sniffed, swirled…you have got the message by now, and then they grimaced and spat it out.

Stephanie sipped hers without a comment. She poured more and sipped away.

'Gentlemen and otherwise. What did you get from that wine?'

They were silent.

Stephanie spoke up. 'What I got from that was farmyard like the first wine but this time I got a lot of bullshit, but it is coming from all of you. You see, my wine is exactly the same as the first one that Ludlow served, the only difference being that I asked a sommelier to gently change the label. You judged the book by its cover and rejected what you thought would make you look less than you would wish to be if you had been honest. If you remember a story about the Emperor's New Clothes, then I am glad to announce to you that I am the little boy who saw the truth.'

There was silence.

Then she added to her speech. 'A maker of excellent wine once replied to my question about what she thought a good wine is. She told me to taste it and if I liked it then it was good. If I did not like it then it was a bad wine for me. Gentlemen, learn to be honest with yourselves and others rather than playing a game of snobbery.'

She turned on her heel and walked away winking at Ludlow who was in on her trick.

20
DIRTY, MUDDY CORPORATE TRENCHES

Gordon's wife had bought me as part of a range of books to occupy him during his 'garden leave' between his old job and a new one with a competitor.

I read him as a good man with a heart of gold who loved his family dearly. We made some sort of bond and I was the book he would look at from time to time during his life. It meant that I could update his story and follow his progress with interest.

Gordon was happy to have his new post. At the age of thirty, he had achieved his ambition of being a Marketing Director for a large international company with its head office in New York. We will call it Brand A.

He had been headhunted from a competitive company, Brand B, and his new employers wanted both his skills and his knowledge of the company they had fought wars with in their attempt to win the biggest brand share for their products.

The problem with wars in companies is that as well as fighting the enemy, the fight often happens within the ranks of the army of executives itself. Dogs of war turn to dog-eat-dog as the skirmishes take place to be as high as possible in the ranks in a grand battle that may be won for a while before the enemy turns the tables and the losing staff get turned over.

Gordon had been told by a cynical member of his team that there were always two plans with his new employer; left drawer and right drawer. If his predecessor had gone for the plan in the left drawer then Gordon should open the right drawer, adopt that strategy and go for it.

As an ambitious man, he wanted his own ideas from his own drawer that bore no marks of copying, reproducing or corporate tactics to retain a job by pleasing the men above him. Yes, it was an all-male hierarchy of macho men who were thought better in a hard battle. No comment about that piece of idiocy.

After his first day, as he drove home in his brand-new Mercedes, he was none the wiser about what his role would be. His job description was written in a cryptic code that resembled little that he had agreed before signing his contract. He felt he was there just to do the grind of getting market share with no approved budget or support from the other directors who seemed to resent his arrival in their world of politics and mystery.

Marketing men were seen as flash talkers, good presenters of crap who wore the best suits possible.

Gordon thought hard about the tactics and strategy that should be adopted. He saw that the brand share war was so similar to the First World War where the fight was for small strips of territory at any cost, usually a very high one in terms of casualties. Nothing was achieved from the swopping of blood-filled muddy trenches.

Brand share statistics were the only measure they had for assessing the gains and losses. They were reported on a monthly basis and in the presentation room it was the main event.

'Brand A has 48% share of the market. Brand B has 52%. The war is being lost.'

A new battle had to be started. The responsibility for the figures rested solely on Gordon. He had been there for just three months and he was seen to be failing already. The figures had risen from 45% but they did not outweigh Brand B.

An American 'corporate colonel', Mathew Johnson was brought in to teach Gordon what to do. He had a small gaggle of assistants who thought they were the experts in the marketing war.

He, unknown to Gordon, approached the main retailers of their product with a cunning plan. They would measure the shelf facings' lengths and ask to be set out according to brand share.

Gordon was being challenged and the explosive mine in his career was about to be planted.

When he talked to buyers for the supermarkets, they explained the plan set out by Mathew Johnson and he was so angry that he complained to the CEO, Steven Shaft, about the proposal. He listened and said that it seemed a great idea. He told Gordon that it was a shame he had not come up with that plan and ended the meeting.

His boss was a British man who was more interested in making money on the side by introducing a new product that was imported from a rogue state in Africa. He had no interest in Gordon's problems in being set up for failure and told him to ignore the Americans and get on with his job. End of story.

The shelves in the supermarkets were reset. Johnson had just used a scheme imported from the American market without any research whatsoever. He was building his career to become a General. He needed to be seen as the trouble-shooter for the headquarters. He wanted to be recognised as a rising star by the big boss. He wanted fame, glory, power and lots of money. People were cheap and dispensable in his own battle for himself.

Two months later, the brand share numbers were presented.

'Brand A has 40% share of the market. Brand B has 60%. The war is being lost badly.'

Johnson screamed at Gordon who put his head in his hands from pure desperation. It was not from a sense of being bad at his job. He had argued against the brand share shelf-space idea but had been overruled by both his boss and this American fame grabber.

What Gordon had discovered when the plan was first mooted was that his brand, Brand A had a 55% share of the shelf spacing thanks to his Merchandising Manager who had negotiated over the past year for the shelf spread in the shops. Based on brand share that space had been reduced. That accounted for the drop in sales. Nobody had listened, nobody had any interest in the views of the man and his team who had worked so hard to bring in results.

Mike Miller took Gordon to one side and suggested that they had a drink that evening. Mike was a subordinate to Johnson and gave the impression that he did not like his ambitious boss very much.

Over the days that followed, Mike and Gordon became friends. Families were involved at dinner parties and days out. Plans were discussed and polished. Gordon was able to write up a stunning plan for building brand share and sales.

He was due to present it at the beginning of the following month, in three weeks' time. He had space at last. Johnson had flown back to the headquarters in New York and would be away for at least two weeks.

A week before his presentation was due, an emergency meeting was called. Johnson had returned from America and was given centre stage. Steven Shaft was distant in his mind. He had problems with the licencing of his product that would make his private fortune. Brand A was the last thing on his mind, but he made the introduction.

'Matt has something to say. Please pay attention. It is a brilliant concept.' He sat down and Johnson stood up to show his importance.

'I will outline a brilliant war plan that will overcome all of the problems we have had to face recently.' He stared at Gordon and paused for half a minute.

'This is what we are going to do...'

He outlined the plan that Gordon had put together and had discussed with Mike. He had been betrayed and sold out by the false friend who was working as a spy for Johnson.

'This plan will be put into action by my colleague Mike Miller who has been a loyal and successful member of my team. I am returning to America where I will introduce these ideas there. We need to build our brand share in our biggest market and I have been chosen to do that by the wonderful President of our company.

All the directors, apart from Gordon, clapped as Johnson sat down. Gordon stood up and, without a word, left the meeting. He had been nothing more than cannon fodder in this war of brands and egos. However, nobody saw his big smile as he left the board room.

He discussed a settlement figure with the two-faced boss after telling him his plan had been stolen by Miller and Johnson. Shaft was not interested; his future would not be put in jeopardy by stirring muddy waters. He went with what was best for him.

The negotiations changed when Gordon said that he would keep silent about the underhand deal that his chief was setting up. The settlement amount increased dramatically.

Gordon packed his personal items into his brief case and called his wife to collect him from a nearby pub.

He called his old CEO and asked for a get-together. At their meeting Gordon explained what had happened. His old boss laughed. 'I told you that they are bandits. You followed what I suggested and it came to pass. They offer spies as friends to find out what their employees are thinking and then steel the ideas and fire them. Seen it happen so many times.'

Gordon replied. 'Thank you for your advice. I took it. In truth, there was a guy there called Mike who I knew was a plant. I told him about a plan I dreamed up in my bath that would destroy the company and kept my real plan to myself. I knew from the start that he was a double dealer. I was inspired by my children who were very critical of the packaging and content of Brand B. Too much plastic, too much sugar and fat. Children are very aware of their health and the health of the planet. You should make some big changes, James.'

After a few moments, Gordon's ex-boss spoke.

'How about coming back to us? Difficult, perhaps, but Harry is leaving us to set up a company that sells camping gear. Different, but it is his dream.'

Gordon had not signed a non-disclosure contract with Brand B and started with his old company as the new Marketing Director after taking a three-week holiday in Florida with his family.

Not only did Brand A change its packaging to paper rather than plastic, it reduced sugar and fat and made a big appeal to mothers who wanted to feed healthier and palm oil free snacks to their children.

Brand B followed the fantasy plan concocted by Gordon and stolen by Mike and Johnson. Their sales slumped after they increased the prices to pay for the bigger packs of recyclable plastic and half-price offers for smaller packs that when bought together were higher priced than the old ones selling more product.

Brand A was unstoppable. Manufacturing was powered by solar generated electricity and the paper packaging was produced from regenerated forests.

And to add salt to the wound, Brand A launched a competitive product to the one owned by Shaft. This time the raw materials would be ethically sourced and it did not take a great effort to share the truth about the use of contraband sourcing for Shaft's product.

This would be a new war but this time it would be general versus general.

In America Johnson ended his career by adopting Gordon's crazy plan and even then, failing to implement it properly. He was undermined by others who resented the arrogance of the man who would not listen and learn.

Mike Miller was recruited to work with Shaft in the new company and spent a long time unemployed after the company went into liquidation after being beaten into the ground by Gordon's superb strategic planning.

When he heard the news, Gordon tapped me gently and put me back into his desk drawer. He had loved the story I had told about trench warfare and the undercover agents used in the first World War.

21
THE COFFEE TABLE

I was surrounded by luxury.

George Peters placed me in the middle of the coffee table made from mahogany that was illuminated by the sunlight pouring through the magnificent windows of the Georgian mansion sitting on the top of a small hill but neatly hidden from the view of 'ordinary' people by tall trees and thick bushes around the perimeter.

He had put me there as a joke as I was sharing the same shiny glass top as hardback books about fashion, antiques, art and historical figures who had lived in the house in the past. They were there to impress rather than for reading. Sir Mallory had invited his usual club of money makers for a Sunday morning meeting that was always followed by a lavish and alcohol driven lunch that brought a little more truth from this band of professional deceivers.

I was looked at and ridiculed by two of the other attendees but not touched by the master of the house. I read, at once, the natures of the two powerful men who were there to connive and plot how their immense wealth could be made even greater. None of them were honest or decent including the man who had received me as a gift from his PA, Debbie. It was her joke and a dig at him for his constant sexual advances that she used as her power over the formidable boss she had. If she gave in then she would lose the titillating advantage she had but she needed to keep him interested in order to receive the huge salary that she was paid. She had to give him hope. Debbie was in the parallel situation of a trophy wife as she followed him at three paces in order to build his reputation as a mogul who had beautiful followers when photographed for the press. Always aware of being blackmailed and vindictive press leaks, her salary bought her silence. That is what I had read in the mind of George. She was climbing the ladder and he was a rung that was in the middle and that she needed to reach the top.

'What is that shit on my table?' Sir Mallory shouted as he saw me. It was not a joke; it was a severe reprimand. I wanted him to pick me up or push me so that I could read him at first hand rather than through George.

The other two men, one by one, touched my cover as if I were a black magic doll and I was shocked at what I read. I was in dangerous company.

The maid brought coffee for the gang and was talked about in derogatory words after she left for not having large breasts and for wearing a skirt that was too long for their needs to lust after a representation of the female role to please men. But through the eyes of George, I could see she was a beautiful woman in her late twenties.

'Rosa, take that piece of crap away, will you.' Sir Mallory barked as if she had put me there. She picked me up and walked away. Even though she was till in earshot, Sir Mallory started.

'I chose her because she is black and they have service for white people in their genes. I would like to bed her but I have no idea where she has been, but maybe one day after she has been checked out by my doctor...' He deliberately wanted her to hear what he said. After she had gone, he continued.

'She represents what the problem is. She is paid too much for what she contributes to the wealth of the country and she takes from the stanchions of the economy. What we need is for less to be paid to the plebs like her and the poor people in the village near this house, and more profit to the captains of businesses like ourselves'. The others nodded their agreement.

'Which makes me wonder about an obvious thing. I can never understand why the captains of slave ships kept them locked up. They should have been used to sail the things. They were free and sailors had to be paid. Awful thinking to not exploit what they had as cargo. You didn't have to feed slaves much but sailors were given food. Waste of resources. And if a few of them fell overboard, it made no difference.'

I found Rosa an interesting person to read. The descendant of slaves herself, she was used in much the same way. Cheap labour rather than free this time round. She was not what she seemed to the fat cats sitting in the lounge she had just left. Her blood pressure had risen and she changed her breathing to calm herself down.

She gently turned my pages and without needing to know anything more about her, I saw she was a caring and gentle soul. Her ancestors had been used and abused by the wealthy who became wealthy from their use and abuse of her forebears, to put the story of slavery into a circle of words.

I found that she was a fountain of information from what she had heard and witnessed in those hallowed halls. She knew more about the gang of affluent felons that they knew she did. Not stupid, not naïve, she was smart. Her beauty was hidden by doing the opposite of the female socialites and sellers of favours who frequented the manor for the pleasure of the men who used it as their secret brotherhood. The men would want her to give her body to them for their thrills. She was not a woman who would do that. She hated them with a vengeance.

I discovered that she knew that some pharmaceutical chiefs were happy to run costings on the profit they would make from cures against the income they received from long-term treatments. And she knew which politicians and civil servants were on the take for their services to oil the wheels for this group of wealthy men.

She was taken for granted and never perceived as somebody who might understand what was going on. 'Too thick for that'. She blended into the place as easily as the fine silk curtains that adorned every room.

She had a secret, however. The stupid maid that she appeared, covered the fact that she had a master's degree in politics and she was gathering information about her employer and his cronies as her ancestors had gathered sugar cane in the past. She was the smartest 'stupid' woman you could meet. She played her role well.

'Where do women have the curliest hair?' Sir Mallory had asked her one day. She acted dumb and embarrassed. He answered his own question. 'In Africa, of course.' He walked away laughing out loud at the 'foolish' servant. She cursed him under her breath as she slowly crept back to her duties. 'And where do rich and hideous men keep their most prized possessions? In their underwear.' She thought to herself and smiled.

On her day off each week she would go to the town a few miles away and meet her boyfriend and tell him all that had happened since their last rendezvous. She was aware that her lover was an investigative reporter who was working on his story about corruption in the economy and who the people were.

Timothy Charles was an honest man who had the hearts of people in his work. He was working in tandem with Rosa to undermine corruption and exploitation. He wanted to become the modern William Wilberforce in bringing about a greater equality in the distribution of wealth and in giving human rights to those whose dignity had been stolen. His notes contained the names of many men and women who had become rich by exploiting others and his story was about to be published.

His deadline was approaching and his files were detailed and his information verifiable by honest men and women in authority. He was not proud of what he was doing, that would have been a selfish pleasure, but he was satisfied that his work would right some of the wrongs in society and trap the users of innocent, hardworking, people. These manipulators of the holes in the law and in the greedy working of those who had the responsibility to make society work as a whole system where all had a share, albeit some bigger than others for what they added.

She put me on his desk in the temporary office he had in a rented house that he used while doing his investigations. He would spend time hiding in the undergrowth that faced the metal gate at the road side of the long drive to the mansion so that he could spot visitors and put their names on his list.

He picked me up and had a quick look. 'I will read this later.' He said, but I had read him already. Apart from the schemers I learnt about from Rosa, there were those law breakers who carefully hid insider trading, lucrative contracts that were way above the costs of alternative offers but less profitable for the team and a whole host of others of the same disgraceful character. The information in his mind about corrupt businessmen and politicians would have made my head spin, if I had one.

Drinks were served before lunch. Aperitifs were given to each man. Rosa bowed and at the back of her head she hoped that they would choke on them. Once the glasses were emptied, they called for more to toast the success of the meeting.

Eventually, the coffee table was about to be exchanged for the dining table. 'One last thing we need to mention is the removal of a certain reporter who wants to break a story about us. His editor has discussed it with him, has obtained his files and we are all mentioned by name along with others. He came here a few days ago and he asked for his fee to be increased for passing on the information. So, gentlemen, we need to make him, a Timothy Charles, plus the maid disappear. The cook will have to serve our lunch,' he winked. The men laughed politely and stood up.

The one thing that I knew was that the newspaper editor had not been spotted visiting Sir Mallory and so Timothy had no suspicions about him being part of the clique.

As stated earlier, Rosa never got to serve lunch. She was apparently taken ill.

I had decided beforehand that if anything happened to Rosa and/or Tim, then I would publish the information in a different book to this one, under a pen name to expose their crooked dealings that made profits from creating chaos and misery for the population they exploited. The real names will be used and copies sent to every newspaper and television news room.

It will be published very soon.

22
CONFESSIONAL

Alistair Davidson was a priest.

His rich deep voice would have fitted well with a Country and Western singer but in his confessional box it was heard in short directional statements, questions and answers. 'Make your confession' and 'Say 20 Hail Marys' would be the norm.

He had me with him sometimes to fill the gaps between the sinners. His story is somewhat disturbing. There are lots of books in the single book, the Bible. I was an outsider.

When Mary Martin arrived, she was known to the priest, not only from her voice but from seeing her in church. She was young, raven haired, small in stature but big in chest. Alistair looked forward to her visits and when she appeared, he would take his tape recorder out and place it next to the screen where Mary would not see it.

'Oh, Father, I have sinned.' She said nervously.

'And the nature of your sin is what?'

'I am responsible for the deaths of three men this week.'

Alistair swallowed hard and checked his recorder was working.

'Oh dear. Tell me the details of your sin so I can decide what should be the severity of your atonement.'

'Well, the first one was in the churchyard behind the grave of the man you buried last week. It was a tender moment with Roger.'

'What did he do?'

'He loosened my clothes then loosened his and we made love so tenderly it was beautiful.'

Alistair asked, 'And the other men? What happened?'

'Well Nigel was actually the first one. We made furious love and he told me he was having a Heavenly time; well that is when he had his heart attack and died. He had a big smile on his face when he went. That is why I thought Roger would be alright to do it next to his father's grave. It was a sort of tribute. I didn't know he would feel remorseful, drink a bottle of whisky and fall into the river and drown.'

Alistair swallowed hard again.

'And the third man?'

'That hasn't happened yet. But it will do very soon. Wait a moment.'

Alistair paused while Mary got up and walked around to the curtain that hid him. She pushed three photographs under the cloth and they were taken by his sweating hand. After giving him time to view them, she pulled the curtain back, lifted her skirt and exposed her shaven crotch to him

She had heard the gurgling noises as the priest looked at the pictures of her naked body but now, with the addition of the exposure of her private parts, she just heard his death rattle and then the noise of his body slumping onto, and hitting, the floor.

She spoke to the corpse.

'You see father, I know what you do. You record my confessions and then get off on them. Every time I come here it is the same. I can sense your slavering at my descriptions of my love making and parts of my body you have never seen until now. I guess that as you are dead, I will not get absolution but it does not matter. I made all of my revelations up. My mother told me all about you in the suicide note she left for me. She talked of the sins committed by the man who married her in the house of God. How you had abused her and made her feel so guilty that all the pleasure she should have had was stolen by you. And it continued by your voyeurism of me by recording what I said.'

Poor Mary, not the brightest star in the sky, had misunderstood her mother's words. She had been referring to her husband, Mary's father, who the poor girl thought was a saint from whose backside the sun shone. Sure, Father Davidson had married her mother and father in his church many years before as part of his duties as a priest. Her father was the abuser of her mother, however.

She picked the photos, hid them in me, grabbed the tape recorder and left the booth. She would read me later after she had sat in shock as she listened to the words of other women in the village as they were pushed into talking in intimate and personal detail about their love lives.

Mary walked to the altar, kneeled and said to the Heavens, 'Well, it looks like we have had the deaths of a father, son and Holy Spirit this week. What should I do?'

Smiling, she made her way outside to call the ambulance.

His funeral was attended by other priests of various ranks, his brothers, their wives and children. His elder sibling had taken over the family farm, the next down became a banker and the choice for Alistair, against his will, was to become a priest. Every day for him was like being subjected to the Chinese water torture.

Every day he would listen to folk with normal lives that were stained by the sense of guilt they had been developed in them from childhood. A confession now and again would cleanse their consciences and allow them to continue doing what they had done before.

Yet for Alistair, he craved the arms of a woman, the joy of having sex with somebody other than himself and he was tantalised by what happened in the world outside his containment. He had given in when he allowed himself to be a friend to Mary's mother when she was in need of a man in her life who did not drink himself into a stupor each night.

Alistair allowed it to happen. He had not lost his faith in God.

He knew in his heart that it had never been there. His life was an ever-repeating chore of taking Mass, naming babies, marrying people, burying others and, of course, listening to the realities of normal life.

His escape was to record the wittering of men and women who had committed adultery. Young and pretty women were asked to describe the events in graphic detail that involved talking about their breasts and genitals. He loved hearing about the guilt of self-pleasuring by the ladies he heard, watched through the screen and recorded.

Mary's false confessions were for unjustified revenge. Nigel had died from a heart attack, true. But it was in the woods when he tripped on a tree root and shocked himself so badly that he died. His son, Roger, had drunk one and a half bottles of whisky that were left over from his father's wake and had stumbled into the fast-flowing water that took him to his death by drowning.

Mary knew this but wanted to use her lies to kill Alistair whose only sin, apart from being a voyeur, was to be lonely and a non-sexual comfort for the wife of her drunken father. He had been her friend; never her lover.

23
RICH AND POOR

It sounds as if I am stating the obvious when I say that people without a lot of money do not have the luxury of buying things like books for entertainment.

Any books that were bought were probably for their children to help them to broaden their education so that they could break out of the trap she and her husband were in.

When Sophie was in hospital, she was next to a kindly lady called Margaret, who I knew. That day, she had finished reading me and passed me over to Sophie to read. Her neighbour looked tired and sad and Margaret wanted to help her. In that way, I found myself next to her bed. She was recovering from her hysterectomy and was in pain. I was no diversion for her but she had read enough of me for me to know her well.

She rested in her bed and worried about her finances and her family's wellbeing now that she was unable to work for a few months. Her husband, young son and daughter depended on her small income which with her husband's pay would feed them, pay the rent and rates to keep a roof over their heads and to buy clothes that were vital rather than just necessary.

A little while after I had become her companion, she picked me up and said, 'I wish you were a cheque book for an account with unlimited funds. Not for me, you understand, but for my children and loving husband so they would not have to live from food banks and he wouldn't have to work at two jobs just to let us survive from day to day.' Tears trickled down her cheeks and a nurse came over to ask if she was alright. 'Has that book upset you, dear?' The young man asked.

'No. I am just fed up with the pain and not being able to see my family. My husband works all hours and is unable to bring the children to see me.'

There were no words that could help her but Bill, the nurse, did his best to cheer her up by chatting for a while before other duties needed to be taken care of.

Later she woke up and saw the red, blue and yellow flowers smiling at her from the vase on her table. Next to them was a big box of chocolates.

Sophie called the nurse. 'These are not mine. Somebody has made a mistake.'

Bill smiled. 'When the lady next to you was discharged, she asked me to give the flowers and the chocolates to you. She said she had no use for them. Her husband gave them to her before he knew she was leaving. He collected her earlier when you were asleep. She asked me to tell you to enjoy them.'

He wandered off smiling.

That evening her husband, David, arrived with the children. He held a tiny bunch of flowers and the children had a small bag of Maltesers for her. Sophie cried as she hugged and kissed her family. 'You shouldn't have. We cannot afford them.' It was what she had to say even though she was touched by their love.

Feeling embarrassed, David apologised. He had noticed the other flowers and chocolates. 'Have you got a boyfriend? Where did they come from?' He was not a jealous man and was just joking.

Sophie explained but David felt like a failure.

After they had left, David worried that he had not done his shift at his second job to make time for the visit and he cried himself to sleep that night after being cheerful and reassuring for his children.

The following morning, after making packed lunches for his offspring and sending them off to school, he walked to work as quickly as he could. On the way he thought about his talents and skills. He used to help out at an art shop during the school holidays and would use the paints and canvasses he was given as part of his payment to create his pictures. He kept them at home and decided to show them to the children the next day.

He dug them out from old bits and pieces that were set to be thrown out to make space and although they were good, they were not able to make him feel proud. He felt disappointed and decided that the next day they would go to the rubbish dump that was a mile away and, on his way to work.

He carried them but was stopped by the man who used to run the shop he had worked at twenty years ago.

'Can I have a look, please?'

David replied that he was in a rush to get to work and the pictures were going to be dumped.

Mr King, his old boss told him to leave the pictures with him and he would dispose of them later. To save time, David handed them over and carried on walking.

Mr King took them to his new shop, a gallery where fine art was sold. He mentally valued them and put them on display knowing that David would not visit a place that sold pictures that were out of his spending capability.

Two days later, as David walked to work at the same time as usual, he saw Mr King again. 'I have been waiting for you. Do you still paint, David?'

'No. I have no time to paint and anyway, I cannot afford the materials I would need.'

Mr King handed him an envelope. 'Come and see me. The address is in the envelope. Come when you can afford the time.' He shook his hand and walked away in the opposite direction to David who had put the envelope into his pocket as he scurried away.

After finishing work at both his jobs, tired and feeling drained, he walked home, then collected the children from the neighbour who minded them until he got home. They ate a simple meal made from the contents of some food bank tins and rested for a while before putting the children to bed. It was another Friday in his life but at least it was pay day.

He took the packets from his pocket but there were three. He opened the two containing money and put it into a jar. The third one, he remembered, was from his old boss who obviously wanted to sell him art materials that he could not afford. Out of curiosity he tore the envelope open. It had a compliment slip from a shop in the better end of town and stapled to it was a cheque for £2000. The slip simply said, 'Thank you, David. Come and see me as soon as possible.' It was signed, Henry.

David shouted his joy so loudly that both children woke up and rushed down to see what had happened to their father. He sounded as if he had hurt himself. When they got to him, tears were running down his face.

'Has something bad happened to mummy?' They implored. They were crying as well.

David answered, his words interrupted by his sobbing. 'Exactly the opposite. Something wonderful has happened to all of us. Tomorrow we are going to see mummy in the hospital and then we are going to town to buy you some new clothes and you can come with me while I see a man in the posh part of town.'

They arrived at the hospital with flowers and chocolates that dwarfed the ones that were there before and they all cried together as he explained what had transpired and about his meeting with Henry King later that day.

Bill wandered over, not so much as to quieten them down but to share their moment of happiness.

'Looks like Mrs King left you more than a book, flowers and chocolates. She left you good luck. Her husband is a rich art dealer, I understand. She did not know anything about you and I told her nothing of your circumstances but there was something in her heart that wished you well and it seems to have worked. As my nursing mentor once told me, it is the cut that heals itself, given time. The stitches just hold the bits together while the body works its miracle of its own accord.'

The following morning David and his children went to the town and visited the art shop. Ushered into Henry King's office, it was as if the children were expected as well as their father. Ice creams, cakes and fizzy drinks were brought by Henry's assistant and then David was given coffee.

'Henry King started the conversation. 'You have talent my friend. As well as the cheque I gave you, I would like you to choose materials for your paintings. This will be done on the one condition that your work will be sold by me from here and with contacts that I have. I will take my margin and you will receive the remaining money on a monthly basis. Sometimes it will be little and, hopefully, at other times it will surprise you. And one other thing. I will commission you to do portraits of some people who you may have heard of. They are wealthy folk with vanities that like to be reflected in a picture that will outlive them. They like the idea of investing in art and nothing is better for them than being the subjects.'

'Mr King.' David replied but was interrupted.

'Henry, please.'

'Henry.' David continued shyly. 'How can I thank you for your kindness and generosity? Can I select what I need today and collect it on Monday evening after work, please? I have promised the children that we will go shopping for new clothes for them.'

Henry King smiled. 'No need for thanking me. It is my pleasure to work with a great talent and, as I have explained, I will profit as well as you. As for the other question, choose what you need and we will deliver it you on Monday morning.'

After the shopping was done, the family went to the hospital to discover that Sophie was ready for discharge. They took a taxi home and David cooked his wife her favourite meal to celebrate the changes that had happened to the four of them.

It was all circumstance, I promise you, dear reader. David became a sought-after artist whose works sold well enough to allow him to quit his jobs and take away the need for Sophie to work and allowed her to heal nicely. They moved to a small house that was theirs rather than being rented and the children went to school each day feeling happy and loved, which they had always been anyway.

The gifts of portraits of Mr and Mrs King that he painted took pride of place in the home of his benefactor and when the family visited the King's house to mount them on the wall, both the women, at the same time, asked if they had met before.

Then, in an instant, they remembered where and smiled.

24
MAKING AN EXHIBITION OF HIMSELF

Marianne knew her husband was having affairs. He would come home from his work tired, possibly hungover and looking exhausted.

Jonathon was always drained and his mood was not good. He worked at exhibitions every few months. Sometimes in Switzerland or Germany, sometimes in the North of England and it was a regular piece of behaviour when he came home.

The usual day for his return was a Thursday depending on where he had been and the weekends after were always the same. They would do nothing. He would drink a little wine and sit in front of the television saying just a few words now and again.

Marianne was bored with him and never accepted his explanation that he had worked long hours that varied from boring to being jolly and cheerful for customers who expected him to wine and dine them in the evenings at expensive restaurants.

She enjoyed the lifestyle his salary bought but she was full of dark thoughts about what he actually got up to. He was a handsome and charming man who was admired by her friends who she then made efforts to keep away from him. Their social life dwindled as their circle of friends became smaller and it would be up to him to organise the occasional dinner parties for those they still knew.

His work was to maintain sales for an international company and visiting customers was part of his duties. He also had to attend and manage the company's exhibitions where the same customers would visit so they could have a break from their routines and enjoy being entertained in return for orders they would place.

In short, Jonathon knew it was an artificial situation that provided an excuse for buyers to have an expenses paid holiday.

He would have liked to have worked a regular week and spend time at home with his wife but his soul had been bought by the company. His pay was in exchange for the work he had to do when others were relaxing and enjoying life.

A typical week for him when he was travelling would be the office on Monday and Tuesday then flying to his destination on the Wednesday to ensure everything had been set up correctly. Then Thursday, Friday, Saturday, Sunday and Monday would be his employment groundhog days.

Every day, he was up early to drive with a colleague in a rental car from the hotel to the exhibition hall around 50 miles away depending in which city that was. That saved his big bosses money when they stayed in cheaper locations at a distance. After parking the car, they walked to the exhibition hall for a tactical meeting that was never necessary. The German owners of the company liked to follow set routines and the main purpose was to get employees in and ready far too soon for the customers who relaxed over breakfast in hotels nearby because cost was never a problem for them.

Then the boredom set in and was a time to chat to others for a few moments before they found excuses to disappear into their booths for yet more coffee to stimulate them into appearing to be awake. They were on the same treadmill as Jonathon.

Eventually, usually around lunchtime, the bigger customers would arrive for a glass of wine, whisky or brandy to give them the holiday spirit while Jonathon and his workmates declined and drank coffee to the extent where it was necessary to make an intake and output decision. Going to the toilet mid-presentation was not considered polite.

Then other sharks would smell the blood in the water and

circle around until the small British team was free and then they would swim in for their drinks and if they got their timing spot-on, an invitation to go to one of the cafes for a salt beef sandwich, beef-burger or the finest bratwurst in a bread roll, depending on where they were exhibiting. At times Jonathon became confused as to his location because they all blended together in his mind to be the same.

Then after lunch the big cheeses arrived to tie up the loose ends of the arrangements for dinner. 'So, you will pick us up from the...name supplied...hotel at eight tonight. See you later.' And they walked away. Matt, his colleague laughed. 'Which day is it, Jon?'

'It is only bloody Thursday. Just four more to go after this one.'

Entertaining friends is one thing, customers another. Jonathon would have a glass of wine, Matt half a bottle, customers a bottle each. That was the routine. Matt was a bad driver sober and Jonathon did not trust him after even one glass so he always drove.

At around midnight, the buyers would be dropped off and an hour later Matt and his boss would find their rooms, crash onto their beds and do their best to sleep until the alarm went off at seven the following morning.

Off they set to work again after a rushed breakfast of croissants, wherever they were. No time for something cooked.

'Which lovely dinner guests do we have tonight?' Matt asked Jonathon who looked in the diary and pointed to two names.

'Oh shit! Them.' That ended the conversation.

The two middle-aged-plus women who they had to entertain that evening were big drinkers and would be sozzled when collected from their hotel.

'I wish they would learn the difference between here and Benidorm.' Matt spluttered sarcastically.

The evening went as expected with the usual sexual banter and the senior buyer hitting on Jonathon who politely rejected her offer with an excuse about having a 'problem down there' as he pointed to his crotch. 'I would ask you to expand, but it seems you can't.' Her shrill laughter at her joke made the other diners turn and give looks of disapproval.

On the drive back to the hotel, Matt and Jonathon talked about the customers. They were big buyers and impossible not to go along with in their ways when they were out of their offices. When seen in England they were professional to the letter and well behaved.

And eventually the week of excruciating work was over and two tired and worn-out men returned to reality away from the trials of commercial life.

'Hi, sweetheart.' Jonathon greeted his wife.

'Bet you had a good time away, again.' Her tone was accusing and critical.

His joking answer did not go down well. 'Fantastic. Party every night, wine, women and song, as usual.' He had explained and described his work routine over and over again and she would not believe him.

He ate a simple dinner that she had cooked and then fell asleep in his armchair. Then he went to bed.

Marianne tidied up and was shocked when she saw a pair of silky panties at the back of the chair Jonathon had been sitting in. She grabbed them and rushed upstairs.

'Christ almighty. I thought I had put them back in my drawer after Greg took them off me last night.'

25
THE PAIN OF DEATH

Writers' block is not a place in Hampstead where authors live.

In his mind, Hugh was a budding author who was awaiting his big break. He was raised in a wealthy family but had no skills that enabled him to work with his father and siblings to earn a living. He would become an author. All he had to do was write a bestselling mystery novel to show his family what talent he had. He had his laptop; he had his partly used notepad tucked into his pocket so that he could jot down ideas as and when inspiration hit him. He was prepared for every eventuality.

One hundred years too late, he had romantic visions of artists and writers gathered in Parisian cafes where they would talk about their creations; would discuss philosophy and drink absinthe and brandy before going back to their garrets to invent a masterpiece in oil or in words on paper.

That is what he needed. Absinthe, but it was almost impossible to get. It had been made illegal in France but the law was changed after limits to the quantities of its active ingredients were added. Hugh researched and found shops in London where it could be bought. It had never been illegal in England.

He bought some, sat with the bottle, a glass and his pad of paper. A pencil is better than a ballpoint, he thought, as he held it in his right hand; had to put it down to pour his drink into the old tumbler he had bought and picked his liquid inspiration up with his left hand. He swigged and waited for the flow of creativity and genius to be brought to him on the tide of alcohol that at first had made him gag as it burnt his throat.

He waited. Nothing. He topped up his glass and drank again.

This time the burning was less aggressive and he lingered, still expecting something to appear as a wonder of imagination.

Then it happened. He would write a murder story that outwitted the law and the villain would kill his opponents in his search for political dominance.

Fantastic. Another drink to celebrate his magnificence and then he fell asleep.

When he woke up, he was on the carpeted floor of his flat and his head was banging. He put coffee on but before it had brewed, he threw up twice in the toilet. He had no desire for coffee but drank some water instead in his attempt to wash away the aniseed taste he had in his mouth that felt as permanent as a tattoo.

After he had returned to a more normal state, he went to his desk. The notepad was full of scribbled writing and he took a long time to decipher what he had noted down.

He had no idea how to murder somebody and screwed up his notes, threw them in the bin and drank his coffee.

Maybe, he thought, a croissant would inspire him to manifest his Parisian inspiration so he walked to the nearby bakers, bought two and walked home again.

He poured another glass of absinthe and sipped it slowly. Then he went to his desk, grabbed his pad and started jotting. The croissant inspired him. It could be a weapon if it were stale and hard. It resembled a Stone Age knife. This would be his murder weapon. He placed one of his pastries on the window sill to go stale and he ate the other one with strawberry jam. Another idea. The jam looked like blood on his sweet tasting treat.

He needed to try his plan out. He needed to kill something using his newly invented dagger.

He had the title for his book already. 'The Croissant Killer'. No, he thought. That would give the method away too soon. It had to be at the end of the book. 'The French Way'. That would do for a working name. He would change it when the book was written.

He plotted. The ambitious politician who wanted to head up the party needed to remove his rival from office by stabbing him with the lethal cake in his abdomen. Then the post mortem would reveal that he had eaten a croissant that had somehow stabbed him through the stomach wall. Artistic licence, he reckoned.

He finished his absinthe and started to type his plot. He would need a cat or a dog to try his plan out. The croissant was still soft so he needed to make a change.

A stale baguette instead. That would go rock hard and would be better than his original plan. He ate the croissant that had been on the window sill and continued to write.

He still needed inspiration. He had written one page so far. The place where he bought the French alcoholic stimulus was too far away so he slept for a while to steady his feet and then went to the nearby shops again where he bought two baguettes of differing types and a bottle of Irish whiskey.

He went back to his keyboard and looked at the screen. Nothing there. He had forgotten to save his work, paltry as it was. He would start again.

The baguettes were sat on the window ledge to harden and the bottle was opened.

Perhaps he would use Irish foodstuffs to kill. He googled and found gur, something made from stale bread. That would do. No, perhaps not. He had no idea how they were made or how they could be fashioned into a lethal tool.

He would have to use the baguettes as his prototypes. All he needed now was a live animal to kill all for the sake of fine literature. He was not cruel by nature but research was always necessary.

Then he decided to freeze the baguettes. That would make them solid and suitable for murder.

Thinking his plot as he cut the ends into points, he popped both into the freezer and waited. He drank whiskey to pass the time and to allow his mind's eye to visualise what would happen.

When he woke up the bread still had not frozen enough. He would have to wait until the morning.

He woke late and reached for the bottle. He wanted to make the most of the day and he was desperate to discover his ingenuity with the type of help the old French writers used. With no absinthe, the whiskey would help, he was sure. Irish writers like James Joyce were known for their great works.

There again, perhaps he should have bought brandy instead, he pondered. He was ready after three glasses and went to retrieve the solid loaves. He mimed how one would go into a man's intestines and as he walked along feeling happy with what could be done with something so simple. He tripped.

He was lucky. His screams were heard by a neighbour who had to smash his door open to see him lying on the floor with a baguette de pain sticking out of his bloody gut.

As he recovered in hospital he was inspired. He knew the frozen baguette could be a workable deadly weapon. He smiled as he started to write his novel titled 'The Pain of Death.' He loved his play on words.

While in the hospital, he was given a copy of me which is how I learnt about the story of a man who wanted to be an author. I smiled in my own unique way at the irony.

26
GARDEN OF ADAM

Eden was very different to Adam's garden.

Adam believed that gardens were for sitting in rather than for spending hours cutting, trimming and taking shoots for new plants. He knew that after all the work, the plants would win by growing back to look exactly like the mess they were in before taking his secateurs, loppers, strimmer and trimmer to them.

The lawn always seemed to need cutting to make it look neat, for humans. It would sigh and then grow back time after every time.

He sat quietly eating a sandwich and drinking a coffee in the bright late summer sunshine. He put me onto a small table alongside his cup and his eyes were caught by the dancing shadows of leaves from his maple tree moving randomly on the patio in some kind of arbitrary way. He stared at them and felt he was being hypnotised by nature.

His mind wandered. He looked the hibiscus plant that had a new flower every day as those from the day before turned dark and withered. Next to them there was a begonia that flowered and kept its blooms through the summer. 'Why' He thought. 'Why does one plant display itself for a day to attract insects for its pollen and then curl up and die, while the others stay there and feed the bees all the time?'

He had no idea.

Then there were tomatoes that were bright red to attract the robbers of their fruit who would eat it, digest everything but the seeds and then dispose of them in chance places along with natural fertiliser. They were symbiotic as were the others. 'Here;

have some nectar for pollinating me. Pick my fruit, eat it and excrete my seeds.'

The system was balanced and it worked for the plants, not for Adam. His prized plants would die and the weeds would survive without water. He asked himself why mankind had not produced plants that lasted by cross breeding them with couch grass? They had made weed killers that would work for a while but the weeds always came back. They even grew from the joints in his patio as if it were the best place to sprout.

Aware that he was being looked at by many eyes, he felt no sense of paranoia. The insects read him and if he tried to squat a wasp then the target would send pheromones to its friends to help ward off the threat which caused more panic, more attempts to squash them and, therefore, even more wasps.

He was watched and read by the lizards in their attempts to label him friend or foe. He had noticed in the past that lizards will attack others of the same species to consume them or if chance allowed escape, a wriggling tail. They could not eat him but any crumbs he dropped from his sandwich would attract bugs that were their prey.

He knew there were snakes in his patch but they were so well camouflaged he was unable to see them and if he went near to them, they would slither away to safety and he knew, would only retaliate if he trod on one or if he tried to pick one up. That was not one of his desires. Instead he walked heavily footed whenever he went near the borders and bushes to give advance warnings of his arrival.

He admired the patience of spiders that floated on the breeze to stretch their threads across huge spaces. From the fence to his garden gate was a distance of at least three metres and a single strand glistened in the sunlight. He felt sympathy and was reluctant to walk where he would break the filament of its silk. 'The spiders catch flies and mosquitoes.' He muttered to himself and his mind awarded them a medal for their hazardous attempts to build their webs.

He saw his retriever dog relaxing in the shade of a shrub and thought about how all creatures were able to detect the motives of others. His dog, Ben, would bark fiercely if a stranger approached yet would bark in an excited way if a visitor was pleasant. He was able to tell good from potentially bad and never expected any reward apart from a tennis ball being thrown.

And on to humans in general. Adam would know when to be alarmed when he saw somebody who looked menacing. Sometimes he was wrong and the man or woman covered in tattoos would be the friendliest person he could wish to meet. The change of mind would happen in seconds. Yet if he saw somebody looking tense as if he wanted to rob him, then his body would respond accordingly with a flood of adrenaline going into his bloodstream to gear up his fight or flight mode. Like a formula 1 racing car, he was on the grid waiting for the lights to change colour and then he would run or do his best to defend himself.

It was strangely ironic that this man who was reading me and who I had read was pondering about the abilities of all creatures on the planet to read others. Hopefully, when he reads this book, he might be surprised that he was read by something that he was looking at and touching. Why? I ask. Everything is aware of everything when they look. They search for meaning, intention and they respond to keep themselves safe or well fed.

Now that his snack meal was eaten and coffee drunk, he wandered into the kitchen, put me on a work surface and then changed into his old jeans.

Adam made his way to the garden shed, filled his mower with petrol and started to cut the grass.

His wife arrived in the garden with a basket to harvest the tomatoes, apples and pears. She was the boss of the green space that rested gently outside the house. She was the real gardener who did the weeding and trimming. She liked being in the fresh air watching her plants grow and flower. Her delight was in having things flourishing that attracted and fed the bees, humming-bird moths, butterflies and other insects. She felt it was part of her deal with nature that she should help to provide for other life so that she could balance it with her enjoyment of the beauty of the creatures she attracted. She felt like a protector of life when she fed the birds from the autumn to the spring each year.

Adam's view never changed from being a spectator rather than a worker. He did his bit to keep the peace and when he had finished cutting the grass, he asked his wife if she would like a cup of tea. Once made, and delivered, he found another reason to sit at the table and relax.

Adam was sleepy and sat at his coffee table that balmy evening, drinking a glass of red wine and continuing to read me. He was happy, he was content. Feeling pleased that his garden looked pretty and congratulating himself for mowing the lawn, he started to have curious thoughts.

He was interesting to read as his ideas hatched like an egg. Crack by crack, pieces falling off the container of a new life and eventually something arrived bewildered, and with a look of wonderment.

He gazed at the fencing around the plot of land he owned and questioned if its prime purpose was to keep him in. He smiled. Or it was to keep others out. It was a wooden barrier that signalled to others to avoid crossing a line as if it were the territorial marking that declared where his space in the world was.

He knew that humans are animals but the language of description separated their behaviours. Did it? He asked himself.

In all corners of the animal world there were analogies for what people were like and what they did. The adders that probably lived in his garden were quick strikers that made them the muggers of this place. A passing mouse would be stabbed with fangs and would soon die. If a larger creature got too close then a hiss might frighten it away but a bite would harm, possible kill it. The mugger, its human equivalent, would wave a knife and if challenged would stab to cause injury or death. And in the larger world it was identical to nations and the use of nuclear weapons. The threat was enough to avoid them being attacked; the cost of retaliation was always too high.

Going back to the garden rather than the globe, he thought the colourful and pretty grass snakes were the constrictors that would crush the life out of their prey. The fraudsters who put pressure on others to squeeze their money out of their pockets and bank accounts. Similar to the spiders that would build intricate nets to ensnare and devour whatever flew into them. It does not matter what they are, they were just a source of income, or in the spider's case, food.

His thoughts were flowing fast. It was as if he had been inspired by what was buzzing around in his head and garden.

The birds were there in differing human forms. The ones that mated for life, like Adam and his wife, and those that liked to find new lovers with the passing of time. Their plumage, like clothing, was there to attract and pull in others who would succumb to the charm of their songs, their courtship dances and the promise of a well-built nest. The requirement of alpha males dictated how they behaved. Big cars, big expenditure to impress; a steak by any other price would still be a steak, but the apparent value represented by the cost is related to the notoriety and price of the restaurant.

The cycle of life is complex. There are animals that eat others and there are animals grown to be eaten by people. More sophisticated as predators, humans farm beef, pork, sheep and chickens to kill without risk to themselves.

In the garden there are plants that are fed to make them more beautiful and there are plants that are fed to make them grow big enough to be eaten. Ants are farmers as well. They protect and cultivate aphids for their honeydew. Symbiosis, that word again. That is how well cared for employees live their lives. And there are wasps that paralyse spiders and lay their eggs so that the offspring can dine on living flesh. Parasitic in the same way that mines use cheap labour to dig into the ground to find and crop noxious substances such as cobalt for an ever-needy and wanting western world.

Adam was getting tired of thinking. He poured more wine and his head churned again. This time he wondered about how beasts communicate. They sing, growl, bark and they hiss. Humans use speech and music but also the sounds that call on them to react. The church bells in the distance told some folk to respond to a summoning to resolve their balance of sin and forgiveness. Pavlovian congregations would go in search of salvation. Pack animals would submit to higher powers by rolling on their backs to expose the weak and susceptible parts of their bodies to admit their respect and fear to bigger and stronger forces. It is like the magpies Adam had seen chasing the buzzards to protect their eggs and chicks in the same way as the spitfires chased Heinkels in the Second World War.

'Hello Adam', any wine left for me. His wife smiled as she sat down.

'Of course, my little collar dove.' He laughed as he filled her glass. ' You look lovely today.'

'Thank you, you slimy toad. I know what you are after.' They both burst out laughing

As the sun set, they watched the bats out catching the mosquitoes that were buzzing around. Adam left his thoughts of nature alone after one more thought. 'Bats help us but we do nothing for them. Shame.'

27
THE BIRDS AND THE BEES

Humphrey was really pissed off with nature as he sat in the garden nursing a hangover. He had put a lot of work into cultivating his plants and pots so that flowers, fruit and vegetables would grow and be harvested. He was angry that he had to unwillingly share his efforts to feed his unwelcome visitors.

Feeling really grumpy, he watched bees sucking nectar and pollen from his flowers.

'Bloody thieves. It would be good if they gave me a pot of honey now and again in return. They are my flowers; they belong to me and you are robbing my assets.'

Now, this might have been funny had he not been shouting at the bees going about their business and if he hadn't really meant it.

He hated the insects in his garden. Wasps were an annoyance as they buzzed around his head, sometimes getting too close for comfort.

Every time he tried to flick one away with his hand or using me as a fly swat, they seemed to call in reserves of fellow conspirators to annoy him even more.

Butterflies would lay eggs on the leaves of his plants and vegetables and the caterpillars they produced would munch away creating big black holes.

Dawn, his wife, walked into the garden carrying two cups of coffee, nodded at her husband and started to cut some flowers to put into vases to decorate the house.

'Surprised there are any left. Bloody bees have been eating them.'

His bad joke was not well received.

'Anything else you want to moan about?' Dawn asked without expecting a sensible answer, but Humphrey started to offload his complaints about how the invaders of his garden were spoiling it.

Dawn was unable to resist getting involved on behalf of the creatures they shared their space with. 'So, you could build bee hives and collect the honey, which is yours, you say. Or we could let them take the pollen and nectar back to their hives and let somebody braver than you produce honey which we can buy in jars.' She pouted sarcastically at her miserable partner.

She continued on as her irritation grew. 'And the tomatoes would not grow unless the flowers were fertilised by the bees so they pay you back for the honey anyway but in a different way. Everything that produces things for us to eat from the garden needs the efforts of the bees and other insects to provide you with apples, pears, grapes and other goodies.'

Humphrey jumped in. 'And, as for the birds, they are even worse at stealing from us. The grape vine we have against the wall is stripped when they reach pea size. They are never allowed to grow for us to eat. The blackbirds are the worst. They are like locusts.'

Dawn drew a deep breath before starting her defence.

'Grapes that never grow big enough for us. The vine is an ornamental thing.' She stated firmly. 'And besides, the birds spread seeds with their manure to grow. The fig bush you have, came from a seed dropped by a bird. We never bought it from a garden centre. It was given to us by nature. Birds eat grapes and other fruits but also bugs that eat plants and vegetables. Sure, bees eat nectar and never bring back honey but they pollenate plants and veg for us.'

Humphrey needed to argue back. 'How about slugs? They eat our strawberries.'

Dawn was determined to win. 'The clue is in the word strawberries. If you could be bothered to put straw underneath the fruits then the slugs couldn't get to them. And the slugs are food for the frogs and birds which are decorations provided by nature that we can see and admire and hear their songs which should cheer up most people apart from the miserable ones like you. And, by the way, tadpoles eat mosquito larvae.'

Humphrey thought he had the winning verbal missile. 'How about wasps. A real nuisance and menace.'

Dawn fired her anti-missile missile. 'Wasps are predators of the bugs that eat your plants. Without them you would lose a big chunk of your crops. You know, my dear husband, we could always replace everything with huge blocks of concrete and then nothing would grow, nothing would visit and there would be nothing for you to complain about.

He had no reply other than to complain that his coffee had gone cold.

She smiled as she asked him what he wanted to blame for that happening.

Dawn looked from side to side as if checking that nobody would hear what she was about to say. She wanted to deliver the knock out verbal blow and smiled as she spoke.

'Remember when we were much younger and we were courting. Your approach was to look for indirect rewards rather than pushing for what you wanted. When you gave me flowers, perfumes or chocolates because you wanted sex, you knew you could forget it. But when you gave me flowers because you loved me, the rewards arrived.' She winked at him. 'It was about sharing, not buying. I could tell by your invisible body and face language what you meant. You got what you wanted from shared love rather than from a single need.

'So, to finish my speech and to make a point, in our garden we get want we want by sharing it with all of the other creatures who pay us back with the results of their work to provide for themselves and us. It is never, and should never be, a selfish act where we complain about what the good earth provides as a combined effort. Did your dad never give you the speech about birds and bees?' She laughed as she turned.

'Now I will brew some fresh coffee and perhaps you could look at the beauty in the garden rather than complain about it. And then, just maybe, you will restore that dashing younger man who stole my heart long ago.'

Humphrey smiled to himself as he allowed his wife's words to sink in. He remembered how much he had neglected their love and vowed to make amends as he picked even more flowers for her to display, with a twinkle in his eye and hope in his heart.

28
ANN ADIEU TO A FRIEND

Dying is something we all know happens but nobody has done it and lived to tell the tale.

Sure, there have been out-of-body stories told but maybe they were dreams and fantasies from a stressed mind while death took a hold and was denied by resuscitation. Who knows?

Ann read me while she was in the last stages of life. She had terminal cancer that had started in her breast and had spread. After chemotherapy was unable to stop its advance, she was in a hospice awaiting the end.

Always a positive person, she recalled her life and enjoyed for, perhaps the last time, her memories of when she was younger with long flowing natural blond hair that had turned grey with age and then was lost completely during her treatment. Even now her beauty shone through and her smile for the staff and her visitors was still as radiant as it had always been

Her life had been so full that it would take a huge book to tell it rather than a short chapter here.

She remembered her days at university where she had studied fine art. She used to joke that after four years, she had only learned how to put her eye makeup on correctly.

The memories of her marriage were bitter sweet. A handsome and bright man had wed her and they enjoyed living in a cottage in the tranquil countryside surrounded by trees and wild plants. One day, however, he came home, packed his bags, told her he had met somebody else and left. The only contact they had thereafter was through their solicitors.

Although heartbroken, she continued her life. Now she was a

graphic designer who worked with companies to put her creativity to good use.

Life went on and she enjoyed being with her friends but she had to wait long years before she met the new love of her life. They were happy together and worked hard in their business.

Then the day arrived when her cancer was diagnosed and her life changed. Lots of treatment and the journey began through the highs and lows of hope and desperation depending on each prognosis she was given.

Yet there was no cure for her and she had to adjust to the fate that awaits us all, but for her, too soon.

As she laid in her bed, she started to think about death itself. Maybe it is a problem sometimes to have an astute mind that hopes for truth in the promises made about Heaven and the hereafter, but logic denies belief in a paradise beyond the pale.

She considered her soul might be the rat leaving the sinking ship of her body. It could be that people with dementia have been affected as their souls have started the migration to their final destination to await the small remainders of their minds to catch up one day.

Then she directed her mind to relive her sweet memories of holidays, warmth of the sunshine, long walks, tastes and smells and her lost love and the new passion she had kindled with her partner, now her husband, who sat at her bedside day after day giving his tenderness, affection and support to the wonderful woman he would soon lose.

She died peacefully and painlessly. When she closed her eyes for the last time, her smile was as radiant as it had always been.

It was odd that when her book, me, was removed by her husband as a memento, a bird's feather was held tightly between two pages. He wondered how it had got there and for what reason it marked a story about the value of friends.

29
OUT OF BODY AND OUT OF MIND

I was a regular hospital visitor. For some reason that I do not understand, visitors delight in giving me as a present as if I am a miracle cure for all ailments. Well, I am not, but I am interested by what goes on in my readers' minds when they are facing stressful and worrying situations.

I will tell you about Godfrey in his own words because that will be the only way in which sense can be made of something which is beyond my text.

*****

The moment of my demise was not a shock. It was death as far as I am aware but it could have been something that has yet to be explained to me.

I had been warned that the operation to remove the blood clot in my brain might go wrong.

I am still not sure if it was an out of body or out of mind moment. Confused and bewildered. Too many colours mixed on a palette. Staggered and hurt. I was dead. I saw my body beneath me. Tubes and bandages. Flowers in a vase wilting as if acknowledging my demise. Nurses and doctors resigning themselves to yet another loss. I could hear them muttering as they sped off to another emergency.

Rather than floating up a shaft of light into a celestial palace, it was like being turned into a piece of space smaller than the size of a bubble in a bottle of tonic water.

No ancestors waiting to greet me as if my death was a surprise birthday party. Thank goodness for that! Not that I had anything against my ancestors but I wanted the after-life to be something different to the cliché we are fed with.

Dying was not what I thought it would be. I was still alive but out of touch with my body, my vehicle for so many years. Now I was living in a different place with extra advantages. Time lost its threat and became another facet of the diamond.

My mind was not in the same state it was and I could perceive a difference. A subtle change in my experiences was present. I was in a different place. What is difficult to explain is how problematic it is to describe what it was like in the after-life, if that makes sense!

My first experiences were those of being in a thick, hazy fog. I saw nothing and I heard nothing. I was a dead man in a sterile world. But like a bird hatching from an egg and becoming slowly aware of its surroundings, my senses started to arrive. Vision must have been there already as I could see the fog from the start but it became more acute as the mist dissolved.

My hearing was good but I was now aware of the tiny whispers that evaded me on Earth. There was, as yet, nothing to touch, smell or taste so I seemed to be stuck in a place similar to when I was in hospital. Fed tasteless food through a drip, being ineffective in feeling my bedding with lifeless hands, and not being able to smell even the universal medical aromas because I had tubes up my nose.

So perhaps I was still in my bed suffering an illusion of my death. I was still alive. But no, I was aware that I had moved location.

I find this frustrating. On Earth, as I shall call the place I left, you can make a call or send a text message advising those left behind that you have arrived safely at your destination. Here there is nothing. I feel like a man looking at fish in a glass bowl.

Strange to say, I had sometimes wondered where I would be

when I died. Perhaps the same void that I was in before I was born. I thought that memories would be lost; they would benefit nobody's pleasure, not even mine. The affairs I had before and after I married, those quick and slow joys that would disappear into the unknown.

I wanted to know where my father went when he left his old body to be disposed of? And my brother, plus a good number of friends. I never heard from them anyway, well when I was alive, that was.

I needed to know if they were floating around in a spirit form or had they gone forever after the memories had faded from the minds of the people who knew them?

Then there was that strange surreal place my mind went to when I dreamt. I visited people I had known, places I had seen and, more oddly, weird places I was familiar with but only because I had seen them in my nocturnal fantasies rather than in real life.

And there were strong memories of times full of gross embarrassment and intense happiness that faded like ice cubes in a drink. Cooling at first, and then converting to bland liquids that were absorbed and pissed out into a sewer with no sense of identity left, just a vague impression of their form.

I wanted to know where I was. The answer that came was, I am where I want to be. Time and space have ceased to be constraints. I have no size; I am just thought. My thoughts give me a body and an appearance based on my memories of how I was rather than on how I am now.

So, I am dead. I am adding all this to my journal, somehow. The notes I have always kept and hidden from nosy readers.

I need to share my experience of being dead by painting a backdrop for you. I had assumed that I would be fixed in age; my wish would have been to be thirty. Instead I am ageless. I am a new-born and an old man all in one. I am able to revisit points in my life at the ages I was when they happened.

I can see my parents as they had been when I was a five-year old about to embark upon my first day at school or as they were when I was having my fiftieth birthday party.

It is weird. I am experiencing as well as seeing and hearing everything. I can play and replay episodes of my life as many times as I want in my little bubble of this new existence.

Well I say bubble, but it is different to that. The best example I can give you is the time I had visited a zoo and had watched, God like, as leaf-cutter ants scurried along clear plastic pipes. They had no awareness of me, and the other people, watching. They were in their own world. I am now like one of those little ants but able to scamper about and watch the others at the same time, but without a sense of time.

I can visit the world I came from, but I am unable to interfere with or influence what was happening. Sadly, I cannot go back and murder Hitler. I cannot warn people about natural disasters but I am able live the events.

Being able to experience things without limbs is strange. It is different to paralysis where you can think without being able to move. The sad parts of my life could be skipped track by track as if playing a DVD with many parts. This is strange. My emotions still work and I can live through my life over and over again.

The location of the afterlife cannot be defined. It will not show up on Google maps. I can tell you where it isn't. It is not on Earth.

Here, there is no concept of time as a fixed dimension. That means that it is impossible to be bored because boredom is time passing with nothing happening.

Yet time can be used as an abstract to create the flavours of human lives as they are lived. This is experienced as if time is passing because events have a start and end. Time is flexible, accommodating and nothing to be concerned about. It is like chewing gum. It can be stretched out or it can be rolled into a small ball. The same is true of distance and space. I can pop up wherever I wish, whenever I want.

I float anywhere in this infinity. I can tour the Grand Canyon; I am able to plumb the depths of the Pacific Ocean.

Time is stretched here as it was condensed on Earth. The revolution of the sun was a day, yet the arrival of light from other planets took light years, an eternity of time that was only relevant when it arrived.

Time and space are like a Moebius strip. That strip of paper that is twisted and joined so if a pencil is held on one surface then it keeps on going until it joins the start point. Both surfaces of the piece of paper are drawn on as if they are just one. Time and space here are like that. Everything is a continuum that has no beginning or end. It is difficult even to use words to explain how it is.

Some repeated dreams that I had when alive are here in full view and in full colour. My living dreams seemed to go to the same places. One was always in France, in a house in the vineyards where I would meet up with my friends and drink wine and laugh. This place exists in this new realm, but some of my friends are missing. I can visit them on Earth, but they have not yet left on this journey, and the future is as resistant to penetration as it had been in the past. I guess that when their little holograms come here, we will complete the scene.

After a while, excuse the expression because there was no sense of time in this existence, I was able to see the essences of other people and things. If I call these little bubbles souls, that makes it easier to talk about. They are everywhere, the souls of people, animals, plants and minerals. How can they all fit?

They are as abundant as raindrops in a monsoon, as plentiful as droplets of water in a thick fog, yet there is space. The infinity of molecules of water in the oceans must have been greater than all the after-lives I encounter, yet they all fitted, and that was within the confines of the planet, and we are now in the greater infinity of the Universe!

They, we, float around as if splendid butterflies. Beautiful containers of the memories of experience as if they are colours of the darkest and lightest shades.

It was a bagatelle. I bounced off people, other animals, plants and minerals. All those things that had experienced a life on Earth.

I can tap into their experiences as well. I realise that they can tap into mine. Here is another concept of good and evil, decent and bad. The others can see the time when I had stolen my cousin's toy car. Worse they can see my infidelities and…well I am not confessing everything here. Perhaps this is part of the sense of judgment that we had guessed at on Earth. The punishment is being so transparent to other souls rather than punishment for wrongdoing from a single supernatural being.

The marriage that I had wrecked has to be examined. Not too sure why, perhaps it is to assuage my guilt. Emotions are ever present. I cannot feel joy within an event that can demonstrate the bad actions of my life.

I discovered that I can make changes that make me feel better. If my life on Earth was fixed like a steel post in the ground, then it was permanent. But if my life was like a tree then I could prune and graft it to look and be different. Of course, this would have no effect on what actually happened but it will change my memories of reality.

Change is to be hated and desired depending upon what it is. My metamorphosis was from a human on Earth to a soul in the afterlife. This is a good thing for me.

No longer bullied by a bully at work, no longer worried about a failed marriage, no longer puzzled about what would happen when I died.

There are changes to my living being that I would like to have made, but that is not an option. What will happen when my wife arrives here is unknown but it is unlikely to change anything. My relationship with her will be fixed, by me, in our happier times. Hers with me would remain bitter, I am sure.

Then, the great differences include seeing my parents as I wish to see them, young and full of life rather than old, infirm and waiting to come here.

I have friends from the past who are happy now, and my brother has lost the problems that beset him on Earth. Everything is good.

My life resulted in me being in a forest in which the original tree was lost. If this is eternity, then an infinite number of events are possible. I could edit and rewrite every bad happening in my life. The nice times would remain, but when they followed a new branch they also changed. For example, not separating from my wife prevented me from meeting and loving the new lover in my old life. If I tried to add her as a mistress, then perhaps the branch would shrivel and die.

I heard a voice speaking to me. It told me to go back because, as it reminded me, I had work to do.

*****

The next thing he was aware of was the sound of a nurse's soft and sweet voice reassuring him that he was fine and that the operation had been successful.

30
THE TROPHY BRIDE

Like the trophy on the shelf that was tarnished, Nancy was showing signs of her age in her face and body, and seemingly with no intellect to make conversation, she was of no value any more.

She read me and I could see there was actually a smart woman sitting in a pointless relationship with the husband she was stuck with.

She was not the sort of woman who used her looks and body to get money from a rich man, she had actually loved Paul when they had first met. She did not know that he was a hard-hitting businessman who had made his fortune from spotting weaknesses in companies and after acquiring them, corrected the faults and built them into profitable enterprises.

Even though he was twenty-five years older than her, Nancy was attracted by his easy style with her, his care for her needs and his sharp wit that made her laugh. In contrast, Paul wanted somebody who looked good to enhance his reputation as a suave operator who could get a beauty through his charm. The bigger her chest and the smaller her intellect the better. He wanted a show piece who would fawn and smile at him in public and be too weak to think about having a younger lover. He was pleased with his trophy bride.

As she was not his equal in his mind, he treated her as a servant and demanded from her what would make him happy.

She was disappointed that her man was not what he had seemed after his smooth veneer wore off and exposed a nasty user of people beneath.

The years passed and he viewed her as nothing more than a piece of flesh that was close to its 'use by' date.

He had mistresses who he did little to hide. He wanted her to feel jealous but, more than that, diminished. They were in his life to boost his flimsy ego and he could not realise that they using him for his money in return for him using them for the short-lived flings he had. He was drawing more and more money from his business in his drive to be seen as a playboy in the eyes of his peers. They, however, saw him as nothing other than a lecherous fool who had no qualms about cheating on his stunning wife.

She took his unfaithful behaviour as a salve that prevented him from demanding sex from her. The love had gone and there she was, his little lady, passing her time in the pool or reading. She welcomed the young girls in his life because it meant he had no sexual desire for her and they were draining his money.

As she was considered stupid, she had the full run of the grand house where he ran his empire. When he went away for a weekend with one of his 'assistants' he used for his pleasure, Nancy would wander into his office and flick through his papers. She was not looking for proof of his infidelity, he never hid that.

What she was doing was checking his business deals and how his company was doing.

Then a phone call, a text and photos of documents would be sent into the ether to one of Paul's associates. He would do what he was being paid to do, by Nancy with Paul's money that he gave her to buy expensive handbags, other finery and beauty treatments.

She was not having an affair with Clive in the beginning, but they shared the same sense of loathing at this Lothario who had destroyed their lives. He had seduced, or in other words bought, Clive's wife and exposed the affair to undermine his business rival. Even though she was the same age as Nancy, he decided that the power he would gain from bedding an opponent's wife was worth it.

After the divorce, Clive had driven to Paul's house to confront him but was met by Nancy in her husband's absence.

He was a year older than Nancy and they had a lot in common including a zest for life and the ability to think of issues away from the complicated roles they had played.

They chatted and talked about how their existences were. Paul had used Clive's wife as a weapon against her husband in order to put stress on him and as a result, his business. Nancy talked about how she also wanted to get revenge on her husband but would not entertain him being killed by Clive. They worked out another way to destroy him.

Nancy was bright as well as being beautiful and she had learnt a lot about accountancy from her father who worked for a large investment company. She knew how to spot the faults in the accounts and she passed the information to her associate in the task of breaking Paul by using the same methods he had with other companies.

And so, after a long period of time, Paul was picked up by the Inland Revenue and prosecuted for fraud. An anonymous informer had given details of how he cheated with his taxes. He never suspected Nancy. She was too foolish to understand what he did, he thought.

Shortly afterwards, his company and personal assets were bought by Nancy and Clive who ran their enterprise together and when that was done, Nancy celebrated by divorcing Paul. Clive moved into the house that Nancy now owned.

They worked hard and the company that was on its uppers became profitable and successful once again.

After they married, Clive smiled when he put a new trophy onto the bookcase.

'This is my symbol for you as my trophy wife.' He laughed. 'You won the trophy for being a clever woman who taught me a lot about running a business. I love you so much, not only for your looks, your figure but for you mighty brain and talent. The schmuck you married thought he was getting a stupid woman who would flatter his need for self-esteem but he missed your talents. He was the captain of a beautiful ship that hit an iceberg whose strength was hidden beneath the surface. Like the Titanic, he has sunk without a trace.'

Nancy and Clive raised a glass of champagne and toasted each other before kissing and settling down on sunbeds by the side of the pool. It was where she had spent lonely hours swimming and studying and improving her knowledge of company takeovers and marketing techniques to improve the business that she would own one day.

For Nancy, it was her last glass of bubbly until she drank some to celebrate the birth of her and Clive's daughter.

31
SO TIRED OF WAITING

Excuse me, but I hope you don't mind waiting for this story to start. You see, it will happen, but maybe not for a while, so bear with me. It's annoying and frustrating, waiting, I know. Sorry about that. OK, let's begin.

Trevor was reading me while waiting at an airport. He was waiting for his flight after waiting for his taxi, the check in and security. He was waiting for something good to happen in his life but he was on his way to see his mother after receiving the call that she was about to die.

And so, he was waiting for, but not wanting, the news of his mother's death after the phone call he had received while he was waiting for his life to turn around and become something that he controlled rather than always depending on others to do something that was necessary for him to move forward. Not only in his career but in his marriage and in his role as a father.

The flight was delayed. More waiting. More coffee, more sitting and reading.

He spent his whole life waiting. Waiting to grow from a child to a man. Waiting for exam results. Waiting to meet a girl, waiting to fall in love. Waiting to marry. Waiting for children to arrive.

Now he was stuck in a place from which rescue seemed to be beyond reach. Every few moments, he looked at his phone to check for news but there was never any.

Finally, the flight boarded. He would have to sit on the plane for two hours, waiting to land. He had booked his ticket in a rush and he was at the halfway point between the flight deck and the tail. The place that was the meeting point for the two refreshment trolleys coming from both ends. He would have to wait for a drink and a sandwich. He yawned and then smiled. The flight's progress did not depend on when he had his snack any more than it was not speeded up by the passengers who rushed onto the aircraft so that they could sit and wait for take-off.

He had no connection with the universe that would have an effect on his mother's state of health that would end her life after the accident.

The flight arrived on time. The pilot said they had made up time because they were given a free slot by air-traffic-control.

He walked off, went straight through with his overnight bag to be greeted his brother who would drive him to the hospital.

When they got there, a doctor with a very serious face walked to meet them.

'Would you mind waiting in the lounge?' He did not wait for an answer and walked away.

An hour later, the doctor returned. 'Thank you for waiting.' He said in a worrying way. 'You can see your mother now.' He walked with them to her private room.

'Hello, boys.' I was waiting for you but they had to operate. I am fixed now and they said although it was touch and go, I will live, and probably for another ten years. You will have a long wait before I die.' She smiled.

Her two sons left her with a promise they would visit the next day. They decided to go to a restaurant to eat well and drink a lot.

'Sorry, sirs, but we are very busy and there will be a wait for a table.' The maître-d told them. 'A waiter will call you when we are ready.'

Trevor burst out laughing. 'That's fine. I am used to waiting. We will go to the bar and wait to be called.' Nothing had changed.

I couldn't wait for this story to end.

32
JAMIE

Jamie sat on the sidewalk in the shelter of a doorway that surrounded the market place where shoppers would buy everything from trinkets to meat, burgers, kebabs and vegetables. When the sun shone, he got too hot. When it rained, he got wet. Yet, this was his home for each day.

'It's a good thing that I am on the walkway because I now I cannot sink any lower, and I am too big to fall into the cracks between the slabs.' He thought to himself as if making his bad life sound better than it was.

He could, as it happened.

Some people gave him a few coins, some spat on him, some kicked his legs. He was lower than most in the eyes of the people who goaded him, hurt him and insulted him. They were either very perceptive or they were out and out bigots and bullies who knew nothing about Jamie's life and circumstances. Those who think they are the wisest are often the most foolish.

He was not there because he was addicted to alcohol or other drugs. He was there because his girlfriend, the mother of his son, had kicked him out.

With no relatives or friends he could stay with, the choice was straightforward. He could either cause a big fuss, demand that his ex would take him back for the sake of the child, or he could live on the streets.

Every-so-often he was moved on by the police and then he would go to the park and sit beneath the tree he slept under and ponder about why his life had turned out the way it had. He was not a violent man. He had not shouted at Melanie and had done his best to support her with his meagre wage before the company he worked for went to the wall. He could not find another job as the world was in a dire financial state.

He was unable to claim benefits because he had no permanent address. The house he had shared with Melanie was in her name on the rent book. He had no fixed abode and now, he had no partner in his life. She had met somebody else and she needed Jamie to leave under the threat of her new man kicking the life out of him.

He would wash in the local public toilets but he was unable to launder his clothes because he had no spares.

The money he begged and was given kept him from starving to death but, in his mind, he was already dead.

On his route between the park and the shopping mall, there was an old paved walkway that was a good shelter from the sun if it was too hot for his comfort. It was there that he met his inspirational friend, Tom.

In the beginning, Tom was very small but after a while, he grew bigger and bigger. Tom was Jamie's name for the tomato plant that was growing against the wall. Its roots were hidden between slabs of concrete but they got enough from their small world to feed the plant so that it grew. It was in competition with choking weeds and Jamie was inspired that it could survive such a hostile environment.

One day, Jamie saw the first yellow flowers seeming to smile at the sun, wanting and needing bees to pollinate it so that it could produce seeds and fruits that would be consumed and transported to other places. This was the way in which Tom found the place where he grew to be beneficial.

Jamie, a bright man who was only short of luck, sat next to his friend and thought about this signal he had received by chance.

He thought and thought and thought again. Even when he sat in his place in the market, he took inspiration from his friend.

When the tomatoes had grown and ripened, he collected them and rather than eat them to settle his hunger, he took most of them to the market place where he sold them for pennies to the stall that sold vegetables.

The remaining fruits were divided into those he ate and those he kept to harvest the seeds to plant. Each day, he repeated this routine and for the first time in a long while, he felt he had a purpose.

The stall holder got used to Jamie arriving with his small but sweet and tasty crop that attracted customers to his counters. He got busy, too busy for him to manage the flow of buyers.

The problem for Jamie was that Tom would soon stop producing tomatoes for Jamie. The season was changing. He told the stall holder that he would soon be unable to supply him but, as he had seeds, he would have more the following year.

A conversation followed in which Jamie was quizzed about his life and how it had turned out to be the way it was.

To cut a short story shorter, Stan, the vegetable man, took pity on Jamie. He had been reliable and had offered his tomatoes every day come rain or shine. He had not approached other stall holders to haggle for a better price and he was not a user of drugs or booze.

He offered him a job conditional on him buying some new clothes and living in a summerhouse in Stan's garden. Another condition would be that he would look after the vegetable plots he had that supplied some of the produce he sold, and, it would be essential that Jamie planted his tomato seeds in the lush soil he had.

They shook hands on the deal with a smile. Stan advanced him enough money to buy the clothes he needed to improve his appearance and Jamie became an honest, eager and friendly assistant who was liked by the customers.

The first thing he did with his first week's pay was to buy a present for his son and walked to Melanie's house to deliver it. He was expecting a bad reception from the woman he had once loved, but she answered the door politely and invited him in.

They talked about what had happened over the last twelve months since they had split and she was almost apologetic. It transpired that her new boyfriend was not a nice man, had resented the child being in the house and he had left soon after Jamie had been evicted.

Melanie told Jamie it had been a mistake and that she regretted what she had done in what she called, 'her moments of madness'.

They talked for hours and Jamie played with his son. When it was time to go, Melanie kissed Jamie on the cheek and invited him back whenever he wanted to see Charlie.

Jamie went back to his new home and thought about what had happened. He chatted to Stan over a beer in the garden and they both knew that given time, given care, perhaps the love Jamie and Melanie had once shared might just blossom again.

'After all, Jamie.' Stan said, 'she has got your young tomato plant in her house. The one you call Charlie. And hey, if you do get back together and have another son, then you could call that one Basil, the perfect partner for Tom.'

Stan pointed at the plot already dug for the next batch of tomato plants.

Stan wanted to expand the hope Jamie had found. 'Seeds find cracks to grow in as well as lush plots. It does not make them less viable but the care given makes them grow.'

They both nearly laughed before they shook hands and went to their own beds. I was in the bedroom already on the bedside table.

33
THE VETERAN

Ernie felt uncomfortable. He was scratching a spot where his glasses had made the bridge of his nose sore.

The tears running down his face felt as if they were eroding a furrow alongside the deep lines made by the wrinkles that showed his age. He knew why he was feeling upset. There was a thunderstorm brewing. Lightning would illuminate the dark sky whilst throwing rain to the ground.

Yet, for Ernie, every night was about darkness. Each night was the same. They would be filled with flashes of bombs, shells and bullets speeding past him, but it was worse when the thunder boomed.

At other times, on nights of celebration that involved fireworks his mind was caught between fear and the need to run away to hide.

And lightning was amongst the worst reminders. Bright sudden light followed by explosions. All unpredictable and impossible to place in a location. Random and fickle, they always put him into a fixed point in his head. They would arrive suddenly and like a child having a temper tantrum, they would make their loud and aggravating presence felt. The sound of hail on the roof would be a stream of bullets banging on armour plating.

Ernie hadn't been a prisoner of War but his thoughts were locked securely in his head behind the barbed-wire of his memories. He had no desire for them to tunnel their way out, he needed them to be hidden. If he told others then he would have to remember what he had sealed into his mental cell.

If he had a penny for every time he was asked to recount his war experiences he would have been rich. If he was given a million pennies for every time he told his story, he would have had nothing. His recall would have been too painful. I didn't have to ask him; I saw the stories in his mind. His memories were like fruit in a bowl going bad. Bananas turning black and mould on satsumas.

He was not sure if his recurrent private recollections were the onset of dementia or a cold bath in the reminiscences of his life before.

War is not like it seems in war films where the hero survives and a few extras get badly wounded or die. The bad guys never lived. The enemy always lost.

His shrapnel was in the form of his recall for him. Sharp, damaging and hidden where it couldn't be seen.

The sound of a harmonica would make him cringe and shake. He was taken from his present-day life to the back of an army truck. Somebody would try to entertain the others by sucking and blowing on that instrument. That, for Ernie, produced the sounds of war that were off the battlefield but equally frightening for him.

Each night, when he fell asleep, the nightmares and memories returned. He did his best to avoid them by staying awake but fatigue always won and took him back to that dark place.

After the war, he hoped that peace would come to his mind but it never seemed to. The night when his wife gave birth to their first child, her screams at giving life to the world were not the noise of creation but they were heard only as the screams of his comrades in arms screeching their pain as they died. His wife's placenta was yet another body bag. All he could do, instead of celebrating, was to let out dismal cries of pain.

I share Ernie's thoughts not to glorify war but, to highlight the horrors that veterans carry with them forever. The war was won for his side but, Ernie as he had been, had been lost.

These were not memories of something. They were a

repetition. He was there again and again and again, every night and day.

Although others thought they knew how he felt, only Ernie and me actually know.

It is difficult to fully explain the anguish of the recurrent nightmares that would not go away. The memories that he had to keep to himself because telling others would just bring the horrors he had gone through, back to life.

34
GIVING TOO MUCH

Ian was a loving man. His friends knew he gave his wife lots of gifts and they were surprised when Linda left him.

'Must have found another man. He will find it difficult to live up to what Ian gave her.' They said amongst themselves.

He couldn't understand how he lost her love. He was very upset with his wife. She had stormed out of the house after he had told her that he loved her. Like his friends, he was sure she was off to meet another man.

He had given me to her as a gift and she had enjoyed reading me. One of the stories had made her think about her life and she talked to Ian about how she felt. She suggested that he read me as well and told him about the story that had made her tell him why she was so unhappy.

He read it and I read him.

I did not like what I discovered as he flicked through the pages.

He gave the book back to her but the puzzle was answered for me.

He had given her lots of things as presents and told her very often how much he loved her. She did not believe him and the gifts he gave were not appreciated.

She had left him for another man, it is true.

Heartbroken, he went to their bedroom and opened drawers, cupboards and wardrobes. Most of her clothes had gone. She must have packed her small world into a suitcase while he was out and she must have sent it to the place she would go to after she left. He knew that the man in her life had probably helped her.

He also found all of the things he had given her. Each one had a note taped to it.

He read them one by one and cried. She was so nasty because she deserved everything he had given her, and he had given her a lot.

The note on a gold bracelet said, 'You gave me this after you had given me a black eye. I did not forgive you.'

'This watch was to hide the bruises you inflicted on me.'

Each note said the same thing in different words.

She had been given offerings for every time he had punched her, slapped her, insulted her, accused her of having a lover. The list was long.

Yes, he had given her a lot of hurt, pain, emotional distress, abuse and damage.

He was an angry and jealous man who thought that he could buy love from this lady after he had caused her pain. She had loved him in the beginning but ended up hating him when he had exposed his true nature.

She was now living in another man's house and was very happy to have escaped. She loved this man she was with, her brother. He and his wife made Linda welcome and they laughed together. She had not chuckled with joy for a very long time.

Ian was miserable. He drank a lot and told his friends what a bitch his wife had been and how he had spoilt her by giving her things she did not want. Ian had not mentioned the bruises she had. They could not understand why she had left such a nice man any more than Ian did.

Linda picked up her copy of me and said to her brother, 'This lovely book helped me to make a decision.' Nigel looked at a gold bracelet on her wrist and asked her why she had kept it.

'No, that is not from Ian. That is from my boyfriend who gave it to me as a sign of affection rather than an apology for hitting me.' She winked at her brother and he smiled. 'He came into my life fairly recently after I had made my mind up to leave Ian for my own safety. He saw me in the chemists buying ointment for my bruises, recognised where they had come from and invited me for a coffee to talk about it. He didn't push me for answers but he listened to me. He was a doctor, I found out later. Our relationship grew over time and it was so different to the one I had. I made my mind up to escape.' Tears trickled down her pretty face and she was comforted by her sister in law. Her life had changed. The new man in her world gave her what she needed, true love.

The copy of me Ian had bought for Linda had gone, so he bought a new one so that he could read again the story that had changed her. 'This bloody book helped her to make a really bad decision.' He slapped me onto the bar counter and stormed out leaving me behind.

35
HER DISCOMFORT ZONE

The book that Sally had read before me was about finding her comfort zone. She was not able to find it. The book was rubbish, she thought.

She had curled up in her chair in front of the window that overlooked her garden. The flowers were pretty and admired by any visitors she had, including her boyfriend who loved her to bits.

Paul would bring flowers which she placed in a vase, muttering to herself that she had rose bushes in the garden and if she wanted roses then she would pick them herself.

One evening he prepared a meal for her. He was a reasonably good cook when he put his to it and he was pleased with what he had made.

She ate it and thought that her mother could cook better than Paul and, to add insult to injury, he had served a French wine rather than a Californian one.

Later that evening, they made love. He was a good lover but he could not reach the standards an ex-boyfriend had set, so she went along with it, faked the right noises and rolled over and slept.

She knew she was good looking because she spent a long time looking at herself in the mirror, adjusting her makeup and throwing away the ones that did not seem to work for her. Paul only wanted her for her looks and her body, she knew. He could not appreciate her intellect and so he was not really worth a place in her life. She was too talented to be with a man like him.

And, without realising the irony, this judgmental woman considered herself to be a good critic and she reviewed audiobooks she got with free codes or Kindles that were free.

She would read or listen to the stories she acquired and would give them one star at the most because they did not live up to her standards. They told her nothing that would improve her life and so they were considered to be bad. Her mind was like a non-reflective surface that absorbed nothing of value so little, or zero, came back.

She considered herself to be an undiscovered talent even though she had never finished writing a book having been plagued with writer's block. And even if she had completed her novel about how a woman found satisfaction in her life with a man who saw her as a beautiful and smart politician, then the publishers would not recognise her genius.

The following morning Paul dressed and said 'goodbye'. He meant it. He never contacted her again. Rather than being upset, she was happy. He was not right for her, not good enough, she thought.

With nothing to criticise she was lost. She only wanted to see things that made her unhappy. Then she was in a good place. She was the type of girl who, if given a million in gold ingots, would complain about the weight.

Her comfort zone was not being in her comfort zone. In reality, she just wanted to feel uncomfortable in her own skin. That made her happy.

36
WRONG AND WRITE

Although they had no connection, Margaret was like Sally in many ways.

Everybody has a book in them, the cliché says. Margaret couldn't find hers. It wasn't writer's block because, after all, she had not put any words onto her pad or her keyboard. She looked for inspiration from the heavens but they were not talking to her.

She wondered if she was facing the wrong direction, consulted her laptop for Feng Shui, turned the desk to face a more inspirational outlook, didn't worry about how her office looked with a misplaced desk and started to write, but no words came.

She had read many books and in her role as a self-made critic, she knew what was, in her mind, bad, and gave one-star reviews to express her good taste. Now, all she had to do was correct the nonsense ideas that others had, and her book would be created.

She worked on the tones, descriptive adjectives, action verbs and rich nouns to describe her hero and heroine, who of course was her.

She built her character up by putting others down and so, in her comparison, the readers would love her alter-ego and her ability to be an author. No not just that, a best-selling author.

She had a few friends, some of them honest, who she asked to read the first and only chapter she had done.

They did not like it. It was dark and self-centred.

I am not sure how it came about. Maybe she had doubts after thinking that I could read her, but she changed her mind after the following dream about a lesson from a successful author.

'You need light, you need positives to happen. Instead of talking about oppressive storm clouds in the sky, talk about how the rains would water the plants that were desperate for a drink in the drought. Describe how the rain drops would wash and clean the dust from the air as happens when you take a shower.

'Mention how the sun would shine afterwards to make the cleaner world glow in the warm brightness. Then the bad characters can see the light after the storm.

'When you are critical of others and their words then it comes back to how you think of yourself. Are you jealous of them for doing something that you cannot and therefore criticize your own efforts? You should write with no boundaries, no comparisons.

'Picasso was a great painter and continued to be even after he had changed his style. He painted what he wanted to create and critics were ignored. I'm sure other artists made their own changes but stabbed the canvas with their palette knives because they worried about the judgments of others. Be yourself, Margaret. Stop criticising others and create what you want. Open the doors of imagination in your mind and just and write for the fun of it.'

Margaret woke up with me on her lap. She had read a few chapters and had decided that I was not a good book, likewise as it was with most of the others she had read. This time, before she wrote her review, she pondered on the words that she had heard in her nap. It was as if I had spoken to her, but not directly, but in her reverie.

She went to her PC to write her review of me, stopped, thought she loved the stories and paused.

Instead, Margaret started to write her first novel that began with a huge thunderstorm in the dry and choking farmlands in the South. The crops would represent the suffering of people and the deluge would be their saviour, the hero or heroine, who rescued the land and the people.

Her imagination opened and the words flowed out so fast that she was nearly drowned in her monsoon of creativity.

When her book was published, some people loved it, but some readers hated it.

'Hey, it's their decision to like it or not. I do not care. I have done what I like and it is for others to choose their opinions.

Critics only voice their thoughts and perhaps they lack the inspiration to match up their opinions to what was intended by the writer.'

Back a few years Margaret had cooked a beautiful roast dinner for Thanksgiving. Her mother in law tucked in and complimented her but added, 'Margaret, this is lovely but you should have tasted the dinners that Auntie Vi used to cook.'

Silence followed until Margaret got up, went to the kitchen and stabbed her chopping board to express her anger.

She knew that different styles of cooking add variation to meals that make them interesting. The idea is not to replicate exactly what somebody else has done, but to make it personal by expanding, trying and making changes that add to the whole thing. That is the way great chefs get their stars. They never duplicate another person's recipes in order to produce an oven ready copy, but they add their individual flair.

Margaret had discovered that to criticise added nothing to her own skills but that it had held her back in her wishes to invent good literature of her own making.

When her book received a one-star rating on Amazon from a woman called Sally, her reaction was a simple, 'What the hell does she know about writing?' and she laughed.

37
LITERARY CRITICS

My first book sold because my readers liked it. Simple.

I, this book, want to do with a publication what Dali did with watches. My unusual and seemingly illogical accounts are here to require the reader to think about their own interpretations of their and others', lives.

I know that literary critics get bombarded with books of different types. They must get tired of doppelganger books that try to jump onto bandwagons. 250 Shades of Grey, 3 Shades of Pink, Pride and Sensibility, etc.

Then there are the written versions of TV programmes and dramas that are tedious for them, I assume. Downton Manor, NarrowChurch, Doctor Why and so on.

Then self-help books like, Help Yourself, the ultimate guide to shoplifting

I am aware how bored and fed up they can become with new books arriving in the post each day.

My first book was considered to be too big, too many pages. That was not my choice but the old publisher did that, so this one is small and to the point. My chapters or stories start without having a blank page facing to add to the page count. It is compact and yet offers my reports of the lives of the readers of my first book. The font size is readable rather than being one size too big to spread the words further like a small spoonful of marmalade on a big piece of toast.

Things are not described in poetic terms. You know what a rose looks like without having it described in lengthy descriptions to give you details of its anatomy.

To explain further, there is no romantic prose in the style that I pick up from readers who get lost in other publications. In their realities, if they see a handsome man or beautiful woman then they have thoughts and feelings that evaluate and make decisions rapidly rather than having lengthy and colourful portrayals that would suit Jane Austen. It is more, 'Wow, she/he's fit' rather than 'His rippling muscles propelled him through the mountainous waves like a battleship hunting down an enemy that was lurking in the misty dark shadows of the stony harbour hidden by the grey of granite.'

I hope you get my point. What I hope my readers would like is something that is based on the value and use of words rather than a big, thick book where the same text would tell the same tales but would be a disservice to the reader and the planet in its waste of paper.

So, for any critics who are reading these words, please be kind because I read you as well and in turn, I could tell your innermost secrets to the world and comment on you.

That is not blackmail, it is just how a book feels when it is skimmed over, not read and is given to another person to reject the hours, days, weeks and months of work put into creating it to entertain others.

A NOTE. By the way, the publisher did not want this piece to be this book but after all, it is not just a paperback you are looking at, it is me as I am reading you and I decide my contents. Above all, please enjoy.

38
THE DREAM MAKER

Making dreams come true is a desire some people have. For others, just having and remembering dreams would be a treat.

Janine wanted her life to change so she would go to bed each night, follow a routine she had read about and waited for her dreams to arrive. If they did, they hid themselves away the next day.

Dreams are like worms. If you do your best to grab one then it slithers back into its hole and disappears to who-knows-where, apart from the worm, of course.

The way to catch them is to dig underneath and lift them out. Dreams are more difficult to capture. The best way to find them is to make them. Relying on your unconscious mind to tell you meaningful stories is similar to trusting your arms to become big and as strong as a weight lifter. Possible but unlikely.

For Janine, dream-making was so important that each night she went to bed and became so frustrated that she found it difficult to sleep and so rarely got her mind to create something, anything, that would entertain or guide her.

She bought dreamcatchers, she tried other positions for her body in the bed, she never drank coffee or alcohol after six in the evening and she did twenty minutes of yoga before bedtime.

Nothing happened other than her exasperation and weariness increasing.

She tried reading, which is how we met, and that didn't seem to help. However, the idea of short stories entered her mind. Each night she would search around for ideas. She would let random thoughts and events influence her in finding the stimulus for a tale, fable or daydream. Daydream, yes! That was what she would do. Rather than wait for her sleeping mind to create dreams for her, she would let the stories write themselves from her own thoughts. Not conscious ones but just letting the words flow by themselves. They would come from a flow of consciousness, like writers and thinkers in the past.

Sleep became an unnecessary thing as the womb and cradle of dreams. So, she would take a few simple and random thoughts to bed with her and write, in her mind, whatever decided to jump out. She might write a few notes on a pad next to her bed so she could remember her thoughts.

Then she found that she could do the same thing sitting in her garden, in a park or on a beach. It didn't matter where she was. The locations might have given her inspiration but the thoughts all came from her mind.

She had found the perfect substitute for sleeping reveries. She could plan things in her life by writing them as if the options were part of the plots and then she could jot down the outcomes. When she read her work then she could find answers in the narratives that she had not known before.

It was to her, as in the cliché, as if the words wrote themselves. Perhaps she should find a genre to focus her work. Crime or love; comedy or tragedy.

Maybe she would write stories as if a book could read the reader. No. That has been done already.

Then she thought that a good set of stories could be collated from her conscious dreams that were already written. If those thoughts had helped her then, surely, they might help others who had problems with planning the next steps they should take in their lives.

She edited the words she had, found herself motivated to write more and put them into a format for publishing.

And here is the answer to how this book was written. A book has no fingers to tap away at a keyboard. It has no eyes to see what has been written. It has to depend on somebody, a human, to do that.

The way it works is simple. My thoughts are picked up by the man who is the so-called author. He thinks he is writing from his imagination but he is actually just typing out the thoughts that I send to him.

In the same way that I read my readers; he reads me unknowingly. Sure, his name goes down as the author because he thinks that the words and ideas are his.

So, in this way which is honest rather than devious, I get my stories into a book for others to read. The purported author is happy because he thinks everything is his work.

The outcome is good for all concerned.

There, you now know how it was done.

39
FIRST AND LAST LOVE

Love can be a very precious thing. I know that. Some people love me as a book but others who do not understand me, do not. Hey, that is their choice to make, not mine.

For Cindy, love was different. She had loved Logan, her husband since they were teenagers and he was her one and only man. He was handsome, charming, had just enough money, not too much or too little to make life comfortable.

Have you ever watched a soap on the television and knew what was going to happen to one of the characters having read a 'spoiler'? There is nothing you can do to change what the scriptwriter has decided. If you shout at the TV set to warn the actor or actress that a murderer is lurking in the shadows, it changes nothing. Even writing to the production company will not save a life in the fiction designed to get viewers to watch the never-ending story.

And so it was for me. Cindy's husband had picked me up about a year after she had read me. If I were human, I would have shuddered, I would have shouted. He was planning her death in order to cash in on her life assurance. He meticulously planned how he would commit the perfect crime.

Whereas, as I told you in a different story, I had killed an abusive man by chance, I felt unable to rescue Cindy. She was a nice lady, I could tell but her husband was bored with her because she was always pleasant, never argued, cooked perfectly and he hated that.

I plotted and planned but it was like trying to change something so far out of reach that I knew that her demise was going to happen. I read his planning that was hidden in his head. Cindy was not a strong swimmer and always disliked the idea of drowning.

He set his scheme out in his mind and he would reassure his wife that she would be safe with him. He thought himself to be good in the water and made her believe she would be safe. He lied.

He would take her on a trip to the coast and then she would swim too far out and get caught in currents that would sweep her away and she would drown. Of course, he would be on the beach and would shout for help to no avail.

He would be distraught and would go into mourning for a long time until he met somebody else with whom he could enjoy a relationship that was fiery and dynamic rather than what he found a dull life with a calm and almost perfect woman.

Irony sometimes steps in. He took her away to the beach resort and waited for his moment. He studied the tides and knew when the optimum time would be to push her out of his life.

They entered the water and he encouraged her to swim alongside him. He was not a strong swimmer, he told her, and she would be safe as long as she kept going alongside him because he refused to take any risks.

They were a fair way out when he pushed her head under the water and she struggled. He pushed her out to the point where he knew the rip tide would take her, turned and started swimming back to shore.

His head was pushed under the waves by something. He was petrified of sharks and panicked. Gasping and struggling, he felt himself being dragged.

Thoughts and visions of a great white flashed through his mind as he was pulled along by the rip tide where the monster had pulled him.

His body was found a day later much further down the coast.

Cindy was upset at losing her husband but was very happy that she had taken swimming lessons to overcome her fear of water. She drank her gin and tonic, and smiled at her swimming instructor who had helped her to dispose of a very mean and miserable husband who could not appreciate what a wonderful woman she was.

Her plan, worked out with Theo, could not have gone better. He was a qualified lifeguard and he just happened to create exactly the same idea as Logan so he could be with his new love.

Cindy read me after Logan died and I saw the missing piece that had entered her thoughts after she had read me the first time.

She had been plotting his murder for a while and I did not know.

40
SWEATING IT OUT

One reader, not a nice man, had a story that I read with a sense of shock and it is told here. Fundamental change took place with him in a strange way that was not predictable.

Twenty years before other problems in his life, almost as a joke, Jack thought he would take part in an old style of ritual that would perhaps give him knowledge of the paranormal that would empower him to get what he considered necessary for his complete happiness; more money and women.

How wrong his thinking was in its intention but not in its result. It involved an unexpected journey through the dark places in his mind that terrified him but which brought about a change that affected everything.

He, Jack Taylor, was not a nice man in the eyes of many. He adored using women for his sexual pleasure and he made as much money as he could in order to live what had been described, by some, as his depraved lifestyle. His popularity was short-lived when he walked away without even looking back. He was not aware of that at the time, but he was now.

Things were going to change. His arrival at a place in the countryside came from a choice he had made to visit a new age style event with people he did not know. He wondered why it was not called the older age. He had heard about the nudity, the women and the ritual of going into a super-heated sauna. His curiosity had been seduced. His misunderstanding about what happened at these events would soon come to light.

On that Saturday evening, as naked as the day on which he was born, he stood in the middle of a field with nine other people making a circle around the crackling fire. Some were dancing and chanting as if to bring the primeaval world into that place.

He had met the man who called himself the shaman a little while before the event started. He expected him to look like a witch-doctor but he was just an ordinary guy dressed in a scruffy t-shirt and jeans.

'Isn't this just a show where women get their tits out and blokes flash their knobs?' He asked.

The shaman was not happy at this apparent lack of politeness and respect for the sacred ways.

'You will think differently afterwards.' He said with a demeaning tone. 'We get naked because they want to expose our minds and souls to the Universe without the hindrance of clothes.'

Mumbo jumbo, Jack thought. It is just an excuse to get our kit off.

He had undressed with reserve earlier, as had the other participants and put his clothes into a neat pile.

Looking around in the dim light he established that men and women made equal numbers if he included himself. They shared a range of ages.

And so, his journey began with a visit to a shamanic sweat lodge and there, unwittingly, his soul seemed to have become stuck in a place where his nightmares came to him for resolution.

He had reviewed the women for any that might be of interest to his libido, his sole motive for most things he did. One in particular caught his eye but she seemed detached and he had no apparent appeal for her. He thought that he would work on her later in the evening.

He was proud of his thirty-two-year-old body. He ran three or four times every week, partly for fitness but mainly to use his body and looks as a mobile sandwich board to be seen by admiring spectators. He was a good height but his padded trainers added a little extra as he jogged along.

He would smile at women as he ran past and hoped they would

respond. Some did but mostly they were caught up in their own races with life. Getting to work, scurrying to collect schoolchildren or rushing to the shops.

Now around this bright fire he scanned the naked female bodies. He felt happy that he had chosen a good place to be. In the ambiguous light offered by the fire at sunset some of them were pleasant to look at, others not, but this was never meant to be a fashion event. For him, this was a catalogue from which to choose a potential lover.

With his heart beating in time to the drum, he was embarrassed and cynical but like a person strapped into a roller coaster ride, he had no choice but to continue.

Crawling slowly, one by one, they all went through the small entrance of the branch and mud construction. Moving around the circular earth bank that doubled as a bench, he sat where he was instructed by the shaman. He closed his eyes and felt his body rebelling at the anticipation of the experience.

When they were all settled, the canvas flap that acted as the door was closed. The leader of this venture said some prayers which meant little to Jack and called for the stones that had been heating over the fire outside.

In the dark, their red glow made them alarming rather than comforting as a warm fire glowing in a hearth would have been at home. They had been told that these stones were used because they would not crack and spit hot splinters when water was poured over them.

After being brought, the rocks were placed into a small pit in the middle of this gloomy space. Water was slowly dribbled onto them. It hissed briefly at the pain. The heat and steam soared upwards and outwards so that he had to catch his breath.

The heat was intense. His whole nature was resisting the extreme stress that it was encountering. His body produced copious amounts of sweat in an attempt to cope. It flowed out of his skin as a warm flood. The high temperatures and humidity made a Swedish sauna seem like a comfortable place to be. The heat and the smell of the hot wooden frame plus the aroma of the sage that had been used to sanitise the lodge combined with the intense odour of perspiration, started to make his mind feel fuzzy.

As instructed, as a novice, he prayed to the East, the South, the West and the North.

And then to the elements of Earth, Fire, Air and Water.

Then to his ancestors.

Feeling foolish and totally out of his depth he followed the shaman's instructions to make his personal entreaty to the universe.

He pondered hard, and partly from desperation, he asked for the resolution of all of his problems, hoping that this was general enough to give strength and power to his selfish need for pleasure and then he sat for a while, flicking sweat from his chest with his hand, to let this request sink in.

He rested in that place but then he found himself disappearing into a dizzy and blank haze.

Panicking, he worried that this was the onset on his death.

He had no control of his fate. It was as if he was being taken over and taken away. He decided to make his exit from this cramped and scorching space despite feeling embarrassed and a failure.

Leaving that hot enclosed place by crawling on his hands and knees, he gulped in the cooler air, stood up slowly and attempted to retrieve his discarded clothes from the heap he had left them in.

As he reached out, he staggered around for a few wobbly moments before he passed out. He fell hard, face first to the earth and plummeted, deeper and deeper, into a new and very, very dark world with his fingers stretched out as if reaching for rescue. They clutched desperately in so much panic that the tendons locked tightly making his hands look like the talons of a bird of prey about to capture its victim.

He was dead, he knew. Yet there would be something worse than death to follow. He could see the entrance to a small and narrow cave in front of him. He crawled through it.

All he could see was a red dome surrounding him, trapping him in an enclosed space.

Then there was just silence, there was no noise.

He saw a figure standing in front of him but this was not St Peter, it was a young, beautiful naked blond woman. He scrutinized her body. Pale, smooth skin and pert breasts. Yet she had a look that scared him to the core. An angel, but not the innocent looking ones in paintings with wings, but an evaluator and critic of his life.

He was still nude, just standing in the cave. He was not concerned because there was nobody else there to see him in the darkness apart from the angel who was as exposed as he was.

There was judgement after all. She spoke 'Your first appraisal of me was in looking at my naked body. Rather than trying to find out who I am. You wanted to see if I am of sexual interest, an object of desire, and that depended upon which portion of me you looked at. That was the most important aspect of me, for you, on our first meeting. Here you are in a strange place, not knowing anything about your situation but you still want to decide whether I would be good to touch and to have sex with. That is one of the many ways in which you have upset people in your life.

'You enticed women into your snare as if you were setting mouse traps. Your charm and your promises were the cheese that lured. Once caught they were hurt or injured by your lack of regard for their feelings. You wanted beautiful bodies as a butterfly collector wants those glorious insects. They catch them, kill them and then pin them to boards for their own gratification. The dead give happiness to the hoarders of the exquisiteness that cannot share life with others because their lives have been broken. If they could speak, they would have nothing but contempt for the thieves of their magnificence and the despoilers of their emotions.

'You used your sexual partners rather than attempting to share a loving relationship. You took without giving anything back. You left them feeling used, abused and dirty while you only had a sense of pride and satisfaction in your seduction and orgasm.

'Love making is a mutual pleasure because the sharing of bodies is satisfaction for both parties. Sex, however can be one sided. If one partner demands sex for their own relief then the other person is left feeling used. That emotion of being exploited will return to the user in different ways.

'If love making cannot be a shared joy then it is necessary to find out why one person is eating the whole pizza and drinking the whole bottle of wine without sharing.'

His apprehension increased. This had not turned out to be a pleasurable experience. She continued.

'By the way, did you not realise that the cave entrance you entered resembles the entrance to a vagina? You have spent so much of your life trying to get into them and now that your whole body has returned to the place where you were conceived and born, you seem uncomfortable.' Her mocking smile burnt into him like a red-hot poker.

Suddenly, he was surrounded by snakes. He panicked. Some people love snakes. He felt comfortable with small constrictors but he was scared of the venomous ones. They can be quick, strike if upset and will kill with their poison given half a chance.

'Fear.' He heard her soft voice say, 'That is what lots of people felt when you were around them. Fear from you controlling their lives financially, emotionally and physically. These creatures represent the dread that people felt in your presence.'

He was nothing now. No limbs, no body but he floated around, invisible to the real world and he had to go where he was directed.

Yet, it seemed to him that those people might have been seeking retribution for the way he had treated them. Floating above women who were familiar to him, he could see the hurt he had given for his use of their bodies rather than the beauty of the love that they had wanted to share rather than give. There were not over many in his mind, he never was a Casanova who had hundreds, but he had taken his small pieces of what he thought was pleasure at the time.

He could see the tears they had shed having been used for sex rather than making love. The grinding and grunting he did was an insult. It could have been any woman lying there giving her body to pleasure just him. After all, they had seemed the same in bed with his eyes closed. Blinded by his requirements he never tried to discover their needs and desires.

They were nothing but soft, sweet smelling bodies of flesh that were there for his enjoyment. The gap between physical and emotional satisfaction had been far too wide for him to comprehend at those times.

The difference between rape and what he did to some women is hard to define. At least at the beginning they had been willing and agreeable but afterwards they would have felt violated by his lack of concern and lack of interest in them.

The woman spoke again. 'On a similar subject, you screwed people financially as well. Your gain, their loss. You used their skills to make money for you without any reward for them. You never worried that the time they spent working was subtracted from the time they should have spent with their families and in leisure. They were nothing but slaves and if they ever complained, then you fired them. Like a Roman emperor just one thumbs-down meant a proverbial loss of living for a man or woman. We will move on.'

Then he could see many rooms as if doors to secret passages

in mind were being opened, one by one.

There was a chamber full of naked and scantily dressed women. Nothing erotic or pleasing was seen by his shocked vision. He had a sense of recognition when he saw them but he was unable to remember their names.

He looked with apprehension at the scenes below and around him. There were women who had been abused as children by their fathers, parental friends or others they thought that they could depend on. They had learnt the false belief that giving their bodies would return them love and admiration from people who told them that it was alright to do what they had been told to do. Sometimes their bodies had been sold to the friends of fathers in return for drugs, money or a perverted gratification.

'Can you see where this is going?' The woman asked. 'The women you used thought that your words and actions were genuine and they gave their bodies to you. You took them and then abandoned them. Is that use or abuse, Jack?'

He witnessed other abuses including the demands that sexual acts were performed for friends which would be watched and filmed for future use, shared on phones or added to porn sites on the internet.

There were young girls who had been forced into prostitution and drug abuse by men who wanted sex and profits from one source. But there were so many sources.

He saw women who were slaves. Trapped in homes to provide services of every nature and their only pay was being allowed to live and to maintain the preservation of their dismal lives.

Then a multitude of rapes of both men and women were happening. There was the spilling of blood and murders of horrific natures.

She spoke again, her voice stern. 'Abuse is always abuse and has no scale of right and wrong. What those children go through and how your conquests felt is the same.

'You didn't break the law but you broke hearts and robbed those ladies of their self-respect and pride. But you were a prick in both senses of the word.'

Feeling embarrassed and ashamed, he considered the high costs, to others, of his zeniths in terms of the nadirs he had provoked in his partners.

Then he saw a man who was shouting vile names at a terrified woman. He was slavering at the mouth. His anger was as intense as her fear. Then he slapped her and threw her to the ground. Jack could feel nothing but dread and alarm. She laid on the ground bleeding from her nose. The man kicked her in the stomach and laughed.

She spluttered words through her tears. 'All I did was spill your beer. I am sorry.' He kicked her again. 'So maybe you will learn to be more careful next time, you slut.' He slurred.

The battered woman wanted to run, she wanted to be free of this tyrant, but she had nowhere to go. Her choices were staying with him or being homeless. This was part of his armoury. He could punch her, slap her and strangle her without a conscience because he thought she was dependant on him for her existence. If she escaped, he would find her and inflict more beatings to punish her. She was stuck in this domestic cage fight. She was a spider in an enamel bath that scurried around looking for a wall to climb before she was squashed.

She was just one of so many. There was so much pain to witness and feel vicariously. So many bruises and broken limbs. So much screaming.

And to follow on in this menu of pain, he saw children bullying other children face to face, fist to face or by text or social media messages that eroded any self-belief they had, even to the point of self-harm or suicide.

Yet even greatly diluted to an insult or a sarcastic word, those failings of mankind hurt to the extreme.

'Can you go there and make it stop?' he pleaded with his guide through this hell.

'I cannot. Abuse is very, very abundant in the world. Although you know that, you can do little to stop it because most of it is outside your life. Once you were nearly a victim of abuse. You know how it feels. Become a champion for the abused men, women and children in the world.

'Do something when you get back to banish the suffering that you have just seen, Jack.'

He felt as if he was back in the first cave and then he was evicted rather than born back into the real world.

He heard a voice. It was no longer her voice, but he heard a man talking to him.

At last, he woke up from his dream, journey or nightmare. He did not know what it had been.

His head was buzzing with the memories of his expedition into his mind and soul.

He seemed to be weak as if the episode had been physical as well as mental. Getting to his feet he looked around. It was still night time, but the full moon gave a gentle muted light.

'Are you alright friend? You were out like a light for about ten minutes.' A male human voice with a heavy accent guided him back to land like an air traffic controller.

'Ten minutes? It seemed like weeks.'

The woman he had noticed from the beginning, who had seemed remote, was sat on the ground nearby. She had the same look of confused realisation that he must have been wearing. She was holding her head as if she had seen the Devil. Like him, she was still naked.

He remembered her as the woman he had targeted for his attention. She was very similar to the evaluator he had just left and he wondered if his mind had transposed her into being his judge in his episode of repentance. After all, his first thoughts at seeing her naked at the fire were solely sexual.

Other people were wandering around looking for their clothes and strolling back to the farm house where they had met.

At the same point, the girl and Jack both became aware that they were exposed and, making silly excuses, they moved off to recover their clothes. She was nude but, for the first time in his life, he felt sympathy for the plight of a woman's nakedness in front of a stranger. Rather than lusting at this beautiful sight he rejected any feelings of voyeurism.

After they had both dressed, they walked back together in silence for a drink of water.

The others were sitting around in the big farm kitchen talking about their experiences. None of them seemed to have been where they had been.

He went to bed and slept, dream free, until morning broke.

After breakfast, as if they were drawn together, both of them walked into the forest at the back of the farm and started talking.

'I am worried.' She said. 'I think somebody had spiked my drink with LSD or something. I had some strange experiences, Jack. It is Jack, isn't it? My name is Eve.'

'I had some strange thoughts as well.' he reassured her. 'And I had taken my own water in a bottle so nobody had spiked my drinks. What happened to you?'

She started to talk about her own journey. Although at first, she was embarrassed, after support from him, she talked openly about her meetings with guides and monsters and how she had witnessed herself being a horrible and selfish person to her boyfriends, bosses and family. He listened attentively and the look on his face told her that he had shared some of the same events and he told her what had happened to him.

And so started a romance that became love and then marriage.

However, the bliss did not last forever, it seems. It was disappointing for me not to read Eve's story as she had gone through the same experience as Jack but he got his copy of me after they had split. It seems, she did not want to be with a man with a terrible track record despite him telling her how much he had changed.

He became a saviour of victims having moved from making huge amounts of money to being a helping hand to others. In return he found the happiness that had eluded him before.

41
A GHOST MADE HER SLEEP WITH A MAN

Rachel felt the touch of the monster before she saw the frightening ghostly face staring at her. She had been sleeping soundly before the monstrosity had appeared.

Protected by her duvet she thought she was safe from any dangers that the world would throw at her.

Warm and snug, the chill from the ghost was a stark contrast to the warmth that Roger, her boyfriend, had shared when he had put his hand on her arm before he went home. Now it was replaced by icy stalactites as cold fingers touched her legs. There was nobody else in the apartment block so her screams went unheard as the frozen fingers moved up her body to her throat and gripped tightly.

She reached for the switch on her bedside lamp but her hand would not move more than a few inches. She could not reach her glasses to see what was happening. She started to cry at her inability to move.

Despite the coldness of the phantom that now smothered her body, she woke sweating and turned the light on. This was a nightmare she had had before in her earlier years. It had been forgotten until this gruesome thought she had experienced in her younger days re-emerged in her head.

Rachel got out of bed, turned on the light, put her glasses on and ran her fingers through her long brown hair as if sweeping the horror away. She slipped on her dressing gown to cover her naked body and searched her bedroom for this apparition not knowing what she would do if she found it in a wardrobe or under her bed.

She phoned Roger who was not happy at being woken in the middle of the night. She begged him to come to her apartment, and after he had dressed, he jogged to see her.

They had spent the evening together at her place and had eaten some spicy food and had drunk a bottle of wine. They kissed just before he left. His hands rested on her shoulders and hers on his hips until she tapped the signal for him to stop. He walked to his apartment just a few streets away.

They were friends but on the advice of her mother, she had not made love with him because it would be sinful before marriage.

Her only sexual pleasures had been self-created with her fantasies and her hands. She wondered if that was a greater sin than having real sex. She wanted an actual lover in her life rather than her imagined one but that was out of the question.

Upon his arrival she told Roger about her nightmare. She suggested that he slept on her settee while she went back to her bedroom to sleep.

Half an hour later he heard her scream and she rushed into her lounge where Roger was. Rachel was sobbing as Roger put his arms around her. Part of him realised that he had seen her bare body for the first time but he still covered it with his to give comfort to her.

'You feel cold, let me warm you.'

He led her back into her bedroom, pulled the duvet back and looked away as she got in.

She pulled the bedding and gestured for him to get in. He laid next to her and started to rub her back. She relaxed and he continued to touch her gently. She was unclothed but Roger was in his boxer shorts.

After she was warm, she was feeling aroused and replaced her previously wandering hand with his.

Roger continued touching her, but on parts of her body that

had not been touched before by anybody before, other than by herself.

They made love and she felt happy but also guilty that she had done so before marriage. She had been told that it was wrong to do so. Roger had gone along with her wishes but did not feel guilty that he had taken advantage of the situation. She was a grown woman who had the right to do with her body whatever she wanted.

They woke as the sunlight poured through the window and made love again.

Rachel talked about how she had been told that lovemaking was something that men wanted for their pleasure and that women had been used by them since time began. She told Roger that he was her first and that other boyfriends had pushed and pushed for her to have a sexual relationship. She had finished with them. Roger had been patient for three months and had never even hinted that he would like to be her lover. She respected that and she knew she was ready to take her fantasies into real life.

Rachel knew that she was slightly chubby and she was embarrassed that she felt her naked body would not be attractive anyway.

Rachel told Roger that she had been told that her body was the temple that was not to be played with and Roger replied by telling her that if her body was a temple it was a great place to pray. He smiled and she smiled back.

That evening they got into bed together again, made love, and slept.

Rachel had another dream, this time about a ghost again. It was her grandmother and rather than being cold and threatening, she was warm and cuddly.

She spoke. 'Rachel, I am sorry for scaring you last night but I wanted you to feel happy with a man who loves you and has been easy-going. I know that you could rely on him to protect you and that all would end well. And by the way, your mother is a hypocrite. She had a good number of lovers before she met your father. I have no idea why she felt the need to prevent you from doing what gave her pleasure. Now decide what is right for you for yourself. The dream or nightmare I gave you was to overcome your inhibitions and to give you an excuse to get him into your bed without seeming desperate for a man.' She chuckled as she faded away.

Rachel woke with a smile on her face. 'Roger, I have just seen a ghost, but a friendly one who scared the crap out of me to wake me up, not from my sleep, but from my over controlled life.'

She never knew whether or not it was the ghost of her grandmother helping her out or if it was her own mind playing games, but she was happy. She always felt closer to her grandmother than she had her mother. Her memories of her were a spectrum from her grandmother being a very young person to the grey-haired lady she had seen in her dream.

She kissed Roger, and yes, they made love again.

I know the unknown creates fear, but from that can come love when trust is found.

42
A DEAD-END OBITUARY

Frank was eighty-two years old and lived in a care village. He was a chatterbox who loved to tell the other inmates about his life. He was once a fighter pilot who had numerous narrow escapes while training and while in a few conflicts. After he retired from the Air Force, he worked in America helping to find advantages in the Cold War, almost a secret agent but never licenced to kill.

He had been married but Nicole had died ten years before he moved into his self-contained apartment in the paradise of having company and a garden to sit in that he did not need to work in. Sadly, his old friends he had known had died so he knew nobody until he met his new friends.

He let slip, but in quiet tones, that during his life he had met and bedded a number of beautiful women but he had never told his wife. Some of them were American, some Russian on his trips away to seek out information about aircraft designs and weapon technology.

He had met film stars, pop stars and had stayed in the Caribbean holiday homes of very wealthy businessmen.

He had been a good swimmer and just missed representing his country in the Olympics after he had been nearly killed by a shark in South Africa.

He was well liked and his friends always welcomed his presence although they were jealous of what he had achieved in his life.

He knew that his time on earth was getting less and less and he planned his funeral with a company that would do him proud.

He was aware that he had nobody in his life who could give his eulogy so he decided to write it himself and record it to be played on the day he would be buried.

Frank told a few people and told more stories about how he was unable to have children after an accident when collaborating with the makers of atom bombs where the uranium had left him sterile.

That tale gave him the sympathy he needed to have a few affairs with women who were too old to conceive anyway.

Rebecca, one of the carers felt affection for this man who reminded her of her grandfather and unknowingly gave him perhaps a little more attention and help than some of the other residents.

She made sure that his things were put away in an orderly and neat way and would be attentive to his life stories.

Everybody was upset when Frank died in his sleep. The funeral was set after the post mortem that said he had died from aged related causes.

Rebecca dressed in her best clothes and was sad when she went to her seat in the chapel and settled alongside her workmates. They chatted about what a wonderful man he was and how rich and fulfilling his life had been. Rebecca told her colleagues, as if confessing a crime, that she had picked me up and put me in her handbag as a memento.

She looked at the few of the other old residents who went to say farewell to their buddy and she smiled at the memory of Frank for some reason she did not know.

The vicar said a few words about the man he had not known and was relieved when the recording started to play.

"Hello to you all. Thank you for coming. Anybody who knew me knew that I liked to talk so I thought I would say a few words at my own funeral."

Like a good actor, he used pauses to good effect having

guessed the reactions to his words.

"I told you many stories of how exciting and enjoyable my life was…none of it is actually true. I told tales I invented to entertain you. In reality, I was a junior manager in a factory that made biscuits. I lived my life in the village with the money I got from the sale of my wife's parents house just before she died."

The mourners were shocked and shuffled uncomfortably in their seats.

"I told many lies. I have even lied about my death. If you look to the back of the chapel, you will see me standing there looking at you."

There was silence as they twisted to look but they saw nothing.

Frank's laughter burst out again. "I got you one more time. Sorry, but I just wanted to think outside the box they have put me in."

He laughed again at his joke as the curtains closed and the coffin started moving slowly towards his cremation, and Rebecca rubbed me as I nestled in her handbag where she had put me after clearing out his room.

I knew that Frank had actually told the truth to his friends but he wanted them not to be envious of what he had done. The lies he admitted to at his funeral were actually the genuine history of his very extraordinary life.

43
PREDATORS AND PREY

Mary was a nice woman. She had a pleasing shape and size. Middle aged and hard working in the office where she was employed as an administrative clerk. She was in the middle of her potential career ladder, having put in hours and hours of effort and work to gain promotions but she was destined to go no further.

Too much countered the chances of her abilities being recognised that can be summarised by saying that she was considered to be different. She was married to a man who was also stuck in his attempts to earn enough money to pay for healthcare and good educations for their children.

Mary relaxed by reading and I was both happy and sad at the same time that we read each other. One of the many things that I picked up from her were the thoughts she had after she read a book about the balance of life and how the small and defenceless were preyed upon. Lizards would eat bugs and spiders but they would be potential prey to bigger lizards who, in turn would be caught and eaten by snakes. They, of course were vulnerable if a bird or bigger serpent spotted them. The circle of life was not round for the individual, it was a straight line with a start and possible sudden end.

Men were clever in their search for food. They kept chickens for eggs and meat. Cows, sheep and pigs were raised in fields that contained them or in pens. That is how the need to harvest protein is satisfied in safety. What did not seem to be justified in any way was the desire to kill for pleasure. Men or women against dangerous creatures with only a high-powered rifle and rangers keeping them safe. Hah!

Nobody eats elephants, rhinoceroses, tigers, lions or other

'trophy' animals.

And it was a wider issue, she knew. Mary was a good-looking woman with a good figure and she attracted a different type of predator who wanted to use her for pleasure as if she was wildlife for hunters. One of the reasons she was stuck in her level at work was that she pushed the men who wanted to have their fun with her, away. She was treated as a useful tool but never promoted to where her pay would increase substantially for the undoubted skills that she had.

She was abused, certainly. A pretty woman was a suitable sexual adventure for the chasers of amusement. An imaginary head to pin to the wall as their plaque to show that the pursuit had paid off with no commitment.

Mary's life and career had been tainted by the range of innuendoes from hints that she was beautiful and therefore attractive to bosses, to outright sexual harassment that included fleeting and lingering hands on her breasts, backside and thighs. Then there were threats of rape. She was in a world where nobody would believe her complaints about those male predators and parasites. They were, and are, bullies using their physical size to intimidate or the use of their power to withhold references if she wanted to move to another company. She could be accused of all sorts of misdemeanours that would stop progress.

They were the wealthy and strong who held the big guns and were experienced at their hobbies of intimidation and ill-treatment.

They expected Mary to do as they requested because she, in their minds, was still a slave who was owned by the masters. She had to do as they wanted. Her ancestors had been captured and added to the work forces for no pay. The predators who had consumed the efforts of black people for hundreds of years. For sure, some had become doctors, lawyers, politicians but their success was still thought of as a freak occurrence and an appeasement that would relieve the pain and agony from the people who were treated differently.

It was more than being a black woman or a person of colour; it was to do with the containment of people who were considered to be weak and of less importance than the powerful. All races and colours lived in physical and/or mental ghettos where they could not escape. Hidden from society until they made loud enough noises to be heard.

As a thought for you. I am a book. Does it matter what colour my cover is? Would you refuse to read it if it was black, brown, tan, yellow or white? The colour of my cover does not affect what is inside. My words could be good or not so good for the reader. The cover has no influence on the contents.

Anyway, how did the story of Mary end? Did she get revenge or was she promoted? The answer to both questions is, no.

I am just sorry that I cannot help people like her or the children in sweat shops making clothes, the sex slaves, the itinerant workers picking crops for next to nothing and the poor in Rio de Janeiro and many, many other victims of the new face of the slave trade. All of those people are treated as inferior without having any rights in the big wide, white world.

44
A CUT ABOVE THE REST

Sylvia was not happy. It was not because she was very overweight, or that she never wore nice clothes and makeup. She was like that because she had no desire to attract other people into her life. Quite the opposite, she wanted to repel and discourage them.

She read fashion magazines and looked at pictures of beautiful women. She used them to avoid doing the things that made the stars, models and other more ordinary people appealing.

I felt the pain as the knife cut its way into Sylvia's forearm. I do not feel pain as such but I am aware when my readers suffer it and I seem to react as if it had happened to me.

She would treat her hurt as if she was cutting the men who had abused her in the past. She would use the blade of the knife to punish her breasts that had given pleasure to the perverts who had touched her as if she had been given to them for their satisfaction. The more she complained, the happier they seemed to be. She slashed her thighs and stomach, the other parts of her that had been part of the onslaught.

The harm she did to herself was an expression of her need to repay those agonies she had gone through at the hands, and other parts, of the perpetrators of her abuse, the assassins of her self-respect and the gentle nature she had once possessed.

Her mind tried to take revenge but the only person she could damage was herself by harming the parts of her body that, to her, were guilty of attracting the men who would take delight in her misery as a result of their own sexual depravity for their satisfaction.

Part way through reading me, as part of her need to distract her thoughts from the fiery cauldron of vengeance in her mind that was boiling over, she turned her fury on me.

With her hands covered in blood, she ripped out my pages, tore them up and set fire to the sheets of shredded paper. Only my cover was left and she stared at it.

Like a miracle of salvation, she had an inspiration. It was not me who had hurt her, although one of my stories had created a reaction. I was an innocent victim of maltreatment, as she had been. She had enjoyed reading me but now I was destroyed, just a shell, an empty thing that had lost its very essence.

Sylvia had chosen the wrong target and apologised to what was left of me. Then she realised that her self-harming was hurting the very thing she had once loved. She remembered that her legs had taken her to beautiful places as an escape from the squalid life she lived. There she would see nice people and scenery. She could smell and touch flowers gently, leaving their splendour intact.

The skin on her stomach was the covering for so many inner organs that were hers and did not belong to anybody else. Those precious body parts had enabled her to survive. All of her was hers and hers alone. Nobody had the right to touch them without her permission, they were not there to pleasure others as had been done from her early childhood.

Cutting, stabbing, scratching and picking her body would never hurt the hurters. Her body that had attracted them like flies to a piece of dead meat, was innocent and needed to be looked after, to be cared for with kindness.

The perpetrators of their filthy and obscene crimes of abuse, including her father, were beyond her reach by punishing herself.

She decided to report them to the police and allow the law to put them away in secure cells where they could never repeat what they had done to her.

She put the knife into the sink and got a cloth from the kitchen and started to clean up the blood from her clothes, furniture and then her bedding.

She had rarely washed after going through a period of cleaning and scrubbing her body as if to erase the touches and emotional staining that was there. Washing now seemed to be a bad thing to do because it was a dirty accomplice to the evil experiences she had gone through when she washed the private parts of her body.

This day was different. Before her change, many times, she had thought about the final cut or whatever else would end her life. Now she knew that nobody had the right to kill her by what they had done. They had no entitlement to stop her from dreaming about a happy life free from the past. It was her choice alone to live.

She showered without obsessive scrubbing or guilt. She then dressed in clean clothes that covered most of her scars and walked out into the world, not to escape her life but to enjoy it. There was no price to pay for a crime she hadn't committed. She had always been the innocent victim.

As she made her way to a new life, she thought that self-harm never hurts the hurter. And the body that attracted the abuser is always innocent and should be looked after with kindness. The person who deserves hurt is elsewhere.

She felt free at last.

To remember her transformation, she put me, or just my remains, the cover, into a glass covered photo frame and put me on her wall. From that point I was not touched again so I lost contact with her.

Maybe, one day, Sylvia will read another copy of me and I will be able to catch up on what I know will be a happy life for her.

45
LIFE IS LIKE A SIMILE

Mark saw life through the eyes of a spectator, not a nasty man who peeped at people in embarrassing states of dress and mind. He just saw the ways in which people lived their lives, but he was worried about how he was considered to be by others.

He worried that this book is like a tape recording that takes down spoken words and thoughts and then tells the rest of the world.

He thought that I am a judge rather than a book to entertain the reader by telling stories. Then he was concerned that I could blackmail him even though he had done nothing for which he could be extorted.

Maybe I am more like his mum who saw him do things but attributed his behaviour to his learning curve about right, nearly right and wrong. She loved him and wanted him to be happy in a world she knew was cruel at times. Her husband, Mark's father, had left her to make a new life with a woman he met on the internet and that added to Mark's sense of being influenced by things outside his life. Just electric signals being passed back and forth between two people who, at first, were strangers but who became lovers for the four months it lasted.

Mark blamed himself for his father leaving. Perhaps he was not good enough to keep the love he craved within the household.

He spoke to the photographs on the wall. The eyes followed him around the room and he was sure that his parents, siblings and ancestors could see him. If he did something that he thought would not get their approval then he would apologise profusely to the pictures. And if he swore out loud, he would blush at the embarrassment he had caused.

He worried about lots of things that involved himself and others. Once, while washing his hands in the sink of a urinal he had splashed water down the front of his trousers and had to spend half an hour in a cubicle while they dried. Then he was concerned that other men would have wondered about what he had been doing for all that time in a private part of a public toilet.

It was for that reason he could never contemplate the idea of playing bowls where it seemed obligatory that the old men had to wear white trousers, the worst possible colour for somebody with a weak bladder.

He couldn't work out if his life was like a simile, or as a transparent screen in a metaphor. Perhaps it was as precarious as a ticket given to him for the maiden voyage of the Titanic.

It made no difference. His life was held prisoner by his thoughts and apprehensions about how he was perceived by others who never actually noticed him at all.

He wanted to know what I thought of him if I could read his thoughts. Reading me added to his sense of being watched but despite his concerns he had to read me from beginning to end in one session.

The irony is that he couldn't see that I am a piece of fiction, or am I?

When he reads this book, perhaps he will find his answer.

Mark, the world loves you and wants you to be happy. Be true to yourself and stop giving a damn about what you think others think about you. They just want you to enjoy your life.

Mark, stop worrying, please. Everything is between you and me.

46
EIGHTEEN EIGHTY

It was fun when Freddie had been younger. He had enjoyed being young. Sunny days on the beach swimming through the waves, more to show his agility and prowess to the girls tanning their bodies in bikinis, than because he enjoyed it.

They would all be still there when the sun set and a fire was lit using driftwood they harvested from the high tide line. The food came out of bags that had been buried in the sand to keep them cool from the heat of the day that would spoil them.

Bottles of beer and cider appeared and the idea was to get the girls to drink enough to make them friendly and less choosy than if they were sober.

Guitars appeared from nowhere, it seemed, and the small crowd of girls and boys sang songs, mostly protest ones to show that the singers cared about the state of the world. The sausages sizzled away and bread rolls were cut to accommodate them when ready. Onions were banned because of the effect on the breath.

The flames and hot cinders lit the faces of the girls to give a bright but soft light that added more warmth to the mood that Freddie was in.

They were jolly. After they had eaten and drunk the dancing started. Freddie was happy that he did not play the guitar because it was impossible to hold a girl and a musical instrument at the same time, and he had a head start over the instrumentalists at the point when the first kiss was attempted, rejected and then returned.

This was the set routine for every Saturday and would peter out on the Sunday after they had all woken up, swum to clear their heads, dressed and set off for their homes, college halls of residence or friends' houses.

Something that resembled that routine but which was different happened when Freddie was older. He, and a few or two, would head to the coastal resorts. They would spend two weeks drinking to extremes They would find girls who wanted to collect stray men as random lovers in the moment. Those belles would then disappear after the sex and then after sleeping late and having a hair or many hairs of the dog, the whole circus continued on the next night.

They were days that he would have talked about when he got home but he could not remember much about what he, his friends and the random girls had done beyond knowing he had drunk so much that his head was unable to recall anything. The fortnight would just be a blank. So different to the much more innocent days and nights on the beach when he was two years younger. That was when there was an atmosphere of romance. The boys and girls respected each other and the intimate events were thought out and more memorable than just getting pissed, getting laid and getting into fights with other roaming drunkards.

Now, as an old man, he was unable to remember the good old days and sat in his chair watching television and reading from time to time. That is how I got to know him.

It was not memory loss due to age but an inability to remember what he called the-good-old-days because he was always so drunk he forgot them as they happened.

Parts of his mind remembered flashes of some of the fun he had, but most of it had been forgotten.

The more innocent days on the beach in the firelight stayed with him because they were not made and erased at the same time. Good memories are good things to have.

47
THE THERAPIST'S THERAPY

Jacob was a therapist who used hypnosis to relax his clients enough for them to allow their thoughts and memories to be unrestrained by the conscious censor that minds seem to possess.

He was brilliant at looking after his clients but not good at looking after himself. He would listen to the problems that he was presented with and would search for the causes and solutions for them.

He was talked about and his practice grew. There were so many people who had blighted lives and he was able to free them from their issues, for a big fee.

His life was good, if you saw him from the outside but he was becoming burdened.

Like a vacuum cleaner, he sucked away the debris from the psyches of so many people and, like the machine, he stored it in a bag in his own mind.

He was arrogant to a great extent, and he refused to have a supervisor to talk to and to empty his basket of information. 'Supervisor?' He thought. He did not need to be supervised, overseen and controlled.

One day, his mental bag of dirt burst. He screamed as the memories of others hit him.

He had a panic attack. It seemed not to have a cause that he could find. It just happened. His heart rate shot up alarmingly, he was breathless and he thought he would pass out.

He knew what it was but not why it had happened.

It passed after a while and on his way home he thought he

recognised a man who had sexually abused him as a child. That had not happened but his look of anger scared the man who had looked at him. The innocent stranger ran away.

After dinner with Stella, his wife, he wanted to vomit, he needed to empty his stomach of the fine meal that had been prepared for him. He made his excuses to his wife and blamed it on a prawn sandwich he had eaten for his lunch.

He usually took the dog for a walk after dinner but he was afraid to go outside the house. He stood by the door sweating and panting. He thought he was going to have another panic attack.

He collapsed in a heap and Stella called an ambulance. She thought he was having a heart attack.

He was admitted to hospital and he was diagnosed for, what was loosely described as a nervous breakdown.

The hospital psychiatrist talked to him and probed his experiences with the mentally unwell.

The conclusion was easy to find. Jacob had allowed the detritus and garbage he collected to fester in his mind rather than cleaning it out on a regular basis.

'You should have had a supervisor…' He was being told off by Dr Mervin Jenkinson, a psychiatrist.

Jacob interrupted. 'But I knew what I was doing, I did not need anybody to watch how I did it. I wanted to be left alone, to cope with my own mental health on my own. My mother supervised what I did, my teachers did as well, and my tutors at university and now my wife asks me about my work because she says she wants to be a help. And, to cap it all, now you are doing the same thing.'

'Jacob.' The psychiatrist intervened to stop the ranting. 'Let us look at the same thing from a different direction. Working in mental health is an occupation that has dangers, as you have leant. Rather than thinking of a supervisor as a superintendent, a controller or a superior, think of him or her as your wingman. The pilot who flies near you to give protection and watches your back. Without one you risk getting shot down. Crash and burn as they say.

'I have somebody that I mentally vomit over on a regular basis. They say psychiatrists are mad. We are not but the ones who are too overconfident to seek help will hit a brick wall sooner or later.'

Jacob was told to rest and recover. He had sessions with Mervin to empty his sack of rubbish and he was allowed to go back to work on the condition that he had a wingman to watch over him.

The change of terminology was pivotal and it was used with his clients who needed to understand the relationships they had with bosses supporting employees.

48
REACHING A VERDICT
(Judge and Jury, part 2)

Barry wanted every pretty woman he could find. He was like a stamp collector but his album was full memories of sexual conquests. It made no difference if she was in a relationship with somebody or not.

'I can still pluck a flower even if it is growing in somebody else's garden.' Was his self-seeking motto. He would pressure women, push them with threats and buy them if he had to.

I was on Fiona's lap. She was reading me. Barry took a £50 note out of his wallet and waved in front of her face.

'What is that for?' she asked as she took it from him.

'That is the price I am willing to pay you for sex.' He smiled and she screamed her refusal at him. 'I am not a whore. You disgust me. Billy is worth a million of you.' She spat at him and kicked out as hard as she could.

Her reaction had touched a very exposed nerve. He had always been rejected as he was growing up and that had made him demand and take what he wanted. He lost his temper. He was very angry as he ran to the kitchen.

It is strange how people think in a crisis. Fiona put the bank note into me almost as a bookmark as she tried to stand up to be ready to fight him off.

He returned in just moments holding the knife he had taken from the wooden holder and stabbed her in the chest from behind the chair before she had got up. She was dead in seconds.

He left quickly, saw Billy coming home. Barry hid while Billy went through the front door. Thinking quickly, he went to the door, walked in and saw Billy nursing his wife. He had pulled the knife out of her chest in an attempt to save her and at that moment, Barry attacked Billy. Then he went outside, phoned for the police and ambulance. He shouted loudly to attract the neighbours.

It was well set up even in a short space of time. Barry had framed Billy and all the proof the prosecution needed was there.

Prints on the knife, Billy with blood over him and a witness, Barry, who had seen the murder take place.

What I knew was impossible to say. I had read all three people involved and I knew the truth but was unable to tell anybody.

It is strange how fate steps in sometimes. The above is the piece that I removed from the earlier chapter about Billy and the killing of his wife.

Joanna is a proof reader who read the first draft of this book and the story struck a note about a case her father, a barrister had worked on and had lost.

As the defence lawyer for Billy, Robert Rice QC knew the evidence was sound and it would be extremely difficult to get Billy off the charge, much to his regret because he believed the story he was told about his client's innocence. After many years in practice he had developed instincts, gut feels, about the guilty and not guilty people he had to defend.

He had been disturbed by Billy's conviction and talked about it, a rare event, over the dinner table and later over a strong drink with Joanna.

When she got my draft copy, she read something that she was familiar with. Even the first names matched although surnames had been changed.

She asked her father to read the story and his smart and astute brain started to think.

The next day he reviewed the forensic evidence. Barry's fingerprints were on the book, me, but he had explained that as having moved it away to help the paramedics when they arrived in case she was still alive.

He was interested by the reports on blood splatter. If Billy had stabbed her from the front, he would have been in the way of blood spurting out. Instead the bloodstains were in front on the carpet. So, as reported, Fiona had been stabbed from the back and if she had, then why was Billy on his knees in front of her?

The prosecution argued that Barry had seen her being stabbed from behind the chair and then Billy rushed to the front of her to remove the knife. Surely, he would have withdrawn it after the first stabbing not from the front to make it easier for him. Doubt was trickling through Robert's mind and then, a big clue was the £50 note. Where was it? It had not been presented as evidence or even mentioned in court.

Robert asked for the book to be recovered and inspected.

He was told it had been checked for fingerprints and having found the sets of the two who must have touched it, no other explanations were needed.

Robert asked for the book, me, to be checked again, this time the interior as well.

There it was. The £50 note with Barry's fingerprints on it as well as Fiona's. Tucked into the pages. It turned out that it had been withdrawn from a cashpoint half an hour before the murder. There could be no other explanation for it being in the book other than Barry had been in the house before Billy had got home. Fiona must have been alive as her prints were on the note inside the book.

At the retrial following an appeal, other evidence about Barry emerged. He had underwear that he had stolen from women, including Fiona. Taken from washing lines or laundry baskets set ready for the washing machine.

And the crowning moment was when the police found some

fibres that matched Fiona's ripped blouse stuck to his clothes.

Billy and Barry exchanged places. One was free the other in jail.

I felt good. Well, as far as a book has feelings.

This part was added into the draft before publication. A happy ending to a very unhappy story.

49
CLOSED BOOK

As you might have gathered, I am not the provider of solutions in a direct way but I can intervene now and again when needed in a roundabout way.

For solutions that fit you it is better to see what has happened to others and then seek for a way to resolve any issues that you have in your own life.

As much as I would want to be an agony aunt, I cannot be one. Agony aunts, like astrologers, talk in general and ambiguous terms that through subjective interpretation seem to fit the person seeking help.

The replies are good for selling newspapers rather than for giving any in-depth help or advice.

The detail needs to be understood in the way that I have read you and know you. It is impossible to understand a person's difficulty from a letter or email.

One last thing. The book may seem short. It is not a long or titanic work but it is like a chocolate gateau, never to be consumed to extremes for fear of over doing it.

This whole idea of a book reading its readers may seem an impossibility but most people reckon that they can read their friends and the other folk they meet. Reading somebody is part of being a human and although I am just a book it does not preclude those talents from me, especially when what I have to say is done with a simple purpose.

It misses out the task you might have to do to evaluate and get to know opportunities and risks within your life. People are complex, I am easy to digest at your own pace. I hope you have found enjoyment with me.

50
WHAT ABOUT YOU?

So, did I discover anything about you, dear reader? Have a look and see how much I know about you. It is up to you to make sense of what I am going to say and how it is personal just to you.

- As you first became aware of me, I kept on seeing a person who means a lot to you.
- When you were younger you had some problems. There are bits of your childhood that you would like to forget.
- You are a thoughtful person who can see the hidden parts of the stories in this book. Some appealed to you more than others as happens in a mixture where some pieces mean more than others. The stories you liked the most touched certain areas of your life or your friends' lives. And I know one or more stories might have upset you, perhaps made you angry.
- Although you tell the truth you are also careful about being too critical of others.
- You have a creative drive and you have produced things in the past that you should continue with to express how you feel about certain situations and people.
- In your life you have hit some obstacles but you have either overcome them or they have dissolved away to nothing.
- You have strong memories that are brought back by certain smells and tastes. You can savour those thoughts when you close your eyes and imagine the senses that are associated with them.
- Likewise, music was a strong influence in your earlier days and it is now. Some songs make you recall parts of your life and bring pleasure to you.

- You have known people who are no longer part of your life and you would like to meet some of them again but there are some you are glad to be rid of.
- When you dream, some of them are interesting but others seem strange and difficult to explain.
- You might be wondering how I could have read your thoughts and feelings before you read or heard me. I do not know how to explain it. For some reason, it just happened. Perhaps you read one of my earlier books or know somebody who did. That is all I can say.
- You want to know how your life will progress but I am not a fortune teller. I just know what I have read about you and your private thoughts.
- And I know you have been able to see the twists in every chapter, including this one.
- Come what may, hopefully we have got to know each other well enough for you to kindly review what you have read or heard. Thank you.

REVIEW REQUEST

And just to finish off, if you have enjoyed this book and would recommend it to others or if you have any comments, please give a review when asked by amazon, Kindle or Audible.

Bearing in mind what has been said about criticism in this book, I would be grateful and very content if you would be kind enough to post a review. Thank you.

With my very best wishes, John Smale.